SOMETHING STOLEN, SOMETHING BLUE

Steve Higgs

contents

THE HEART OF WINDSOR

I was in my kitchen fixing a sandwich when my phone rang. It was just after noon on a Friday, and I'd eaten a light breakfast which left me hungry by lunchtime.

Knowing the call could be from a potential client, I abandoned my half-made sandwich and went to where my phone chimed and buzzed at the other end of the kitchen counter.

It wasn't a client after all. The incoming call was from Edward Smallbridge, a high-end jeweller I'd known for many years. Were circumstances a little different, he and I might be dating.

My name is Felicity Philips, by the way. I'm a wedding planner. I used to boast that I was 'the' wedding planner, but I recently lost the opportunity to helm a royal wedding – the joining of Prince Marcus and his fiancée – to a rival and I wasn't entirely sure where that left me.

Thumbing the green button to connect Edward's call and then the speaker button so I could continue to make my sandwich while talking, I said, "Hello, Edward." I could guess why he was calling – to rekindle what had almost started more than a month ago in London. We attempted to have dinner together, but a man I ... hmmm, what's the right word here? A man called Vince Slater interrupted out evening.

Vince Slater is a security specialist and private investigator who I met when he was hired to help a family whose wedding I was engaged to manage. The wedding itself didn't go to plan and I haven't been able to lose Vince since.

He claims to be in love with me and made sure to scare off Edward. To be honest, I'm still not sure how I feel about Vince. He is handsome and has a good body which are big plus points when you are in your twenties. I, however, can boast five and a half decades of life and need more than a strong jaw and trim waist to capture my interest.

We have been on a couple of dates, initially because he coerced me and then because he saved my life and I felt somewhat obligated. We have kissed and nothing more. Vince wants more, but I'm not ready to even think about it, and do I really trust him? He is an utter rogue.

And here was Edward, a man I respected and trusted. On paper, if I were looking for a man to enter my life, he was the obvious choice.

"Felicity," Edward blurted my name, his voice filled with panic. "I need your help!"

Holding the phone with my left hand, my right flew to my chest where the emotion behind Edward's statement was making my heart unexpectedly hammer.

"Edward, whatever is it? What's the matter?" I could not recall ever hearing the jeweller sound flustered before. He was calm and in control at all times; a masterful figure in a hand-cut suit.

"It's the Heart of Windsor!" he stammered. "It's gone!"

My brain needed a moment to process his words and make sense of them.

"The Heart of ..." realisation hit, and I gasped. The Heart of Windsor is a crown, one worn by many a princess over the years. Actually, or more accurately, I should say, the Heart of Windsor is the giant sapphire mounted in the centre of the ornate headpiece. "How?" I asked, boiling all the clamouring thoughts in my head down to a single word.

"It was stolen!" Edward squeaked, the poor man sounding like he was having a heart attack. "I think I know who did it, but I dare not say the name out loud."

"What are the police doing?"

"The police? I can't call the police, Felicity. That's why I called you!"

I blinked, a frown creasing my forehead. He called me rather than call the police? What did he expect me to do?

"I don't follow."

3

"Well you're a sleuth, Felicity."

I laughed, "I'm nothing of the sort."

"Yes, you are, Felicity. Look at how you caught Jessica Bishop when she killed all those people at the wedding fayre. She made the deaths look like tragic accidents, but you caught her."

"She almost killed me, Edward. I stumbled around blindly accusing everyone but her. I thought Primrose Green was behind the murders."

"Yes, but you got her in the end. And that's not the only case you've solved recently. The papers made a big thing out of Rudyard Kipling going berserk. You caught him too."

I got what Edward was saying, but he couldn't be more wrong. My sleuthing skills were non-existent. I was terrible at deducing the truth by examining the clues. Honestly, I didn't even notice the clues. Were it not for my cat and dog, I wouldn't have solved any of the recent mysteries.

"I'm sorry, Edward, but I'm really not the detective you think I am."

"Please, Felicity," he begged, which startled me. Edward was a master in his domain; a man filled with rightful self-confidence. I doubted he ever begged for anything, yet here he was, verbally grovelling at my feet in the hope that I could come to his rescue. "I don't know who else I could call."

My immediate response was that he ought to be calling the police and failing that an actual private investigator. I'm a wedding planner. I

4

didn't say that though. Edward is an old friend of mine. One who has done me many favours over the years and was kind enough to give me the early nod that a royal wedding was coming down the pipe.

Okay, so I didn't get the contract for the royal wedding, but that had nothing to do with Edward.

Failing to give him a response either way prompted Edward to repeat his plea.

"Please, Felicity. At least come to my shop so I can tell you what I know."

My nineteen-year-old niece, Mindy, strolled into the kitchen, making me conscious that our phone conversation was no longer private. Wiping my hands on a towel, I took the phone off speaker and put it to my ear.

Mindy made a face to show she wasn't attempting to eavesdrop and went to the fridge.

"Okay," I relented. "Are you there now?" A trip into London wasn't what I had planned for my afternoon, but recently returned from the States where Mindy and I ran a wedding on board a cruise ship, I was between engagements and didn't really have anything I needed to do.

"Yes, I am," he exhaled a huge sigh of relief. "Thank you so much, Felicity. I promise it will all make sense when I can tell you a little more. I just can't say too much over the phone."

I thought he was being overly cautious, but if he felt there was a need for secrecy, I wasn't going to push him for more detail now.

Edward's urgent need for action pushed him to ask, "How soon can you get here?"

I flicked my eyes to the clock on my oven. It's not that far to get into London, but traffic is always slow around the capital and his shop is right in the heart of the city.

To give an answer, I said, "I will leave shortly, Edward. Expect me by two."

He thanked me again, quite profusely in fact, and finally cleared the line.

Mindy closed the fridge door, a chicken drumstick in her mouth. Tearing a chunk off and chewing, she asked, "Was that Edward the jeweller? He sounded flustered."

"He thinks someone has stolen one of the royal crowns."

Mindy's eyebrows took a hike up her head.

"And he wants you to help figure out who took it?"

My stomach complained about its state of emptiness with a roar like two humpback whales mating. Pressing a hand to my core, I finished putting my sandwich together and took a bite.

"Edward says he knows who took it." I replayed our conversation in my head as I chewed. "Something like that anyway. He might have said he suspects he knows."

Mindy's eyes gleamed. "So we're taking the case? Being a detective is sooo much more fun than planning weddings."

I couldn't help but frown. Planning weddings is my life and I am very good at it even if I do say so myself.

"We can take Amber and Buster," Mindy suggested, clearly enthralled at the concept. "They will be happy to help."

TALKING TO MY PETS

Amber, asleep in a cozy nook by the kitchen window cracked an eyelid.

"Happy to help?" she questioned.

Amber is my ragdoll cat. An odd quirk I cannot explain allows me to hear her thoughts and words. The same is true of my bulldog, Buster, and they can both understand me. It's just those two and it started a short while after I got them. I had the same thing with my pets when I was little, but my parents refused to believe me and gave the animals away when I wouldn't change my story. My older sister, Ginny, denied that she possessed the same ability and taunted me cruelly for many years.

Amber opened her other eye and stood up. Leaping to the floor, she pushed her front legs out and lowered her chin in a stretch that made her body twice its original length.

"I will not be happy to help. However, depending on what you need me to do, I might be convinced to participate."

Mindy knew about my quirk and watching my face guessed I could hear Amber.

"Is she saying something right now? Did she just volunteer?"

"Not exactly." Buster would volunteer. He's a dog and therefore always keen to help. Cats are somewhat differently motivated. "She said she could be convinced to participate."

Mindy looked at Amber, confused. "What does that mean?"

Amber came out of her stretching routine and crossed to rub her face against Mindy's legs.

"It means if the dumb humans want to employ the cat's skills, they have to pay the price."

A squawk of outrage came from my living room, my sister's thumping feet echoing on the floorboards.

Mindy is my assistant as well as my niece. I was a little dubious about hiring her, but did so because I have no children of my own and wanted my successful business to continue with a new generation. At nineteen she is easily distracted but has managed to learn enough about what we do to become an asset. She is also a skilled martial artist which has proven useful on more than one recent occasion.

At five feet nine inches tall, she towers over me, especially when she puts on big heels, but then most people are taller than me. She gets the height from her parents – my older sister, Ginny, is four inches taller than me, and Mindy's father stands over six feet.

Mindy and Ginny are currently living with me, a situation that resulted from Ginny ignoring and generally abusing her husband for the entirety of their marriage. The arrangement was temporary so far as I was concerned, though my sister didn't appear to be doing anything to find somewhere else to live. Truthfully, I believe she was waiting for her husband to 'come to his senses' and beg her to move back in with him.

I doubted very much that would happen. Ginny stormed out when he cancelled her credit cards and raged at how much money she spent while sitting around earning none.

"He did it again, Felicity! You have to get rid of him!"

The him in question was Buster, of course, and the thing to which my sister referred was almost certainly the expulsion of gas from his backside. Little did she know Buster was doing it on purpose because she doesn't like him.

Calmly, I replied, "I am not getting rid of my dog. You might wish to remember, Ginny, that he lives here, and you do not."

"Oh, that's right. Rub it in." She stormed into my kitchen, opening the fridge and closing it again having retrieved a chilled bottle of white wine. She hadn't bought the wine, but she was going to drink it. "It's not my fault I'm living here, is it? It's not as if this is what I would choose."

"You could try apologising to your husband and see if he will take you back," I suggested.

"Ha! Fat chance! He'll come grovelling soon enough."

It had been three weeks already and to my knowledge Shane was yet to send so much as a text to his wife. He was talking to Mindy, and they had gone out to dinner more than once because my niece gets on great with her dad and Shane is a good person. Unlike my sister.

Drinking from the bottle, Ginny asked, "Can't you at least change his diet? What do you feed him to create a smell that bad anyway?"

Buster chose that moment to wander out of the living room. His face is a near permanent grin, but that's just what it does when he isn't displaying an emotion. He trotted up to Ginny and we all heard the hissing rasp of escaping gas.

He ran away when Ginny aimed a disgust-fuelled foot in his direction.

Dropping my plate into the sink, I swallowed my last bite of sandwich and ran. I might disagree with Ginny about more or less everything, but she wasn't wrong about my dog's gas and I wasn't hanging around to savour it.

Buster's amused chuckle sounded in my head.

"I got her good that time!"

I caught up to him and snagged his collar.

"What have I said about leaving smells in the kitchen?"

Buster looked ashamed for about a second before his grin returned.

"*Yeah, but I got her good, didn't I?*" he raised a front paw for me to high five and I just couldn't resist slapping my hand against it.

"You did," I replied. "I would say well done, but let's leave it at that, thank you. Now, how would Devil Dog like to come on a secret mission?"

Devil Dog is Buster's alter ego. I know, right. The daft mutt has it in his head that he is a superhero crimefighter and even puts on a deep, husky voice when in his Devil Dog persona. I don't know if other dogs are like this, but I can report that Buster has asked repeatedly for a utility collar that can deploy a laser gun, and a cape and cowl combination that will cover his face and help to keep his true identity secret. I worry a kennel that converts into a helicopter might be next.

I am yet to make enquiries at the pet store, but suspect such items are probably bespoke.

Buster spun on the spot, his stub of a tail whipping back and forth too fast for my eyes to track.

Rising to my feet, I said, "I'll take that as a yes. We're leaving in a few minutes."

"Who are you talking to?" asked Ginny.

"My dog," I called back, heading into my bedroom to change outfits. Before she could say anything on the subject, I chose to add, "People talk to their pets, Ginny. It's a perfectly normal thing to do."

Expecting a barbed reply, I was surprised not to get one.

From my wardrobe I selected a thin cashmere jumper that would go nicely with my jeans. I wasn't dressing to impress anyone, but I like to know I look the part when I go out. I have a lot of celebrity customers and it wouldn't do to visit Edward's 'by royal appointment' jewellery shop on Oxford Street in dowdy clothes – anyone could be there.

I had to go around Buster as I moved across the room to the mirror to check my hair and makeup.

"*What's the mission?*" he wanted to know. "*Will I be fighting hordes of ninjas? Will there be need for weapons because I've been thinking about a design for a club you can attach to my tail.*"

"You would hit yourself in the face," I assured him, tucking a stray strand of hair back into place.

"*I would practice first, obviously.*" He was completely serious.

To shut him up, I told him where we were going and why, finishing with, "I doubt very much there will be any investigating to do. I am only going because Edward begged. He is flustered and cannot think clearly, but I'm sure he will do the sensible thing and call the police when I calm him down."

Happy that I looked as good as I could without using an iron to take out the wrinkles by my eyes, I called for Buster to follow and almost bumped into Mindy as I came out of my bedroom.

She had changed too. My niece can typically be found wearing stretchy gym clothes which she prefers for their comfort and the ease with which she can move in them. That's what she was wearing just a few minutes ago. Her new outfit of skirt, blouse, and jacket with tights and heels was what I expected her to wear to work in my little boutique in Rochester High Street.

My eyebrows wrinkling, I asked, "Are you coming with me?"

Buster said, "*Yay!*"

Mindy shrugged. "If that's okay." she lowered her voice, "I mean, I don't want to stay here with mum. All she does is moan that dad still hasn't called and refuses to listen when I assure her he isn't going to."

I had no reason to deny her the chance to escape my house. Saying as much, I sent her to fetch Amber and let Buster outside to 'water' the fence.

My regular car is a Mercedes SL two-seater convertible. It's sleek and black and fun to drive, but not exactly intended for transporting pets. I also have my late husband's old car, a restored Ford Escort Mexico from 1972. It ran and handled beautifully and though it wasn't a car I would ever buy or even look at, I knew it was a modern classic and driving it always reminded me of Archie.

It was the more practical choice with the pets in tow and already had Amber's cat carrier and Buster's seat harness fitted in the back.

From Mindy's arms where my niece carried her to the car, Amber voiced her disapproval at the suggested travel arrangement and promised she would just sit on Mindy's lap.

I argued. "If I leave you free to move about, Amber, you will start a fight with Buster. You always do."

"*That's because he's an idiot and he slobbers. He's a slobbery idiot. I suppose I could have just said 'dog' instead.*"

Buster exposed his teeth. "*How about I remove your tail?*" he asked. "*I'm sure you would look better without it.*"

"You see what I mean?" I pointed to the cat carrier. "You need to ride in there. There's a nice, comfy blanket for you to sleep on."

"*I'm not going in the carrier,*" Amber stated with a tone of finality. "*Either I ride on Mindy's lap or I'm not coming.*"

Now, I could just stuff her into the carrier, but then getting her to do something helpful later would be all but impossible no matter what I offered as a bribe.

"*Put Buster in the boot,*" Amber suggested. "*It's where he belongs.*"

Buster lunged for her, barking and snarling. He wasn't on his lead and could have torn or muddied Mindy's clothes if she wasn't so swift on her feet. Sidestepping the enraged dog, she used a foot to pin him to the ground when he landed and that allowed me to put him in the car.

15

I was done trying to negotiate with my pets. Once Buster was strapped into place and couldn't get to the front, Mindy got in with Amber and I cupped the cat's chin to make her look at me.

"If you provoke him, I will put you in the carrier and place it so you are next to his bottom."

Looking horrified, Amber spat, "*You wouldn't dare!*"

I narrowed my eyes. "Try me."

Surprisingly, the journey into London was peaceful and I got to chat with Mindy for once.

A RIGHT ROYAL ROBBERY

I parked in one of Edward's private spaces at the rear of his shop, thankful that I was able to do so because there is nowhere else to park anywhere near Oxford Street.

Thinking we would have to walk around to the front and enter through the customer door, I was surprised to find Edward rushing out to meet us. He was sufficiently on edge to have been watching his CCTV camera for my arrival.

"You brought your pets along?" Edward inclined his head in question.

I had Buster on his lead and Mindy carried Amber, now in her cat carrier though she was not happy about it.

Buster employed his silly, gruff superhero voice, *"Devil Dog is here to save the day. Fear not, tearful mortal."*

Ignoring my dog, I said, "You know I rarely travel without them, Edward. Circumstances dictate that I could not leave them at home today." *With my sister who might rehome them while I am out.* The truth was that if I were to attempt to figure out what could have become of the famous jewel, it would be my pets who did a goodly portion of the investigative legwork.

Edward chose to let it go. "Please come inside, ladies. Thank you both for coming at such short notice. I apologise for interrupting your weekend."

I really wasn't sure what to say; he looked so stressed. Edward had his right hand out for me to shake, but I pushed it to one side and pulled him into a hug.

"It will be all right, Edward. Try not to worry." I broke the hug almost straight away, not wanting to linger and make it weird; I still suspected he was trying to propose during our dinner a few weeks ago and we'd never even been on a date prior to that night.

He thanked me and led us both inside, Buster huffing along excitedly at the front.

"Are the bad guys still here? Will I have to fight them? Devil Dog is ready, just don't get too close because all around me is a circle of pain."

Amber sighed, *"Good grief."*

The rear door was guarded by two large men in pressed white shirts and black trousers. They didn't carry guns - this is England after all – but their belts were adorned with other weapons such as those

18

extendable baton things and a Maglite torch which I understand can be a useful tool in a fight. The rear of the building was also covered by CCTV cameras and required a palm print on a biometric scanner to gain entry, plus a code which Edward entered only after making sure the keypad was shielded from our view.

Buster sniffed at the door, waiting for it to open. "*I can smell an evil presence,*" he growled.

"*You can smell your own stupidity,*" remarked Amber. "*Or your face is, as I have often said, far too close to your bottom.*"

I shortened Buster's lead, keeping him close by my ankles so he couldn't attack the cat. At home or in private I would have chastised the pair of them. With Edward within earshot, I didn't wish to make myself look like a crazy person pretending to have a conversation with my pets. It's one thing to talk to animals as I pointed out to Ginny, but another entirely to have people hear you respond to what they believe are my imagined responses.

With one hand on the door, Edward paused and turned to face me and Mindy.

"I need to ask that you don't say anything to my staff. They don't know about the theft, and I would rather keep it that way if at all possible."

Questions arose, though I chose to keep them to myself for now.

The front of Edward's Oxford Street jewellery shop was as plush as one might imagine, but the area beyond, which I had only seen once or twice in the past, was a drab collection of storerooms and offices decorated more than a century ago and never touched since.

The odour was of dust and metal polish or cleaning fluid. I wasn't sure precisely what it was I could smell, only that it reminded me of my grandmother employing me to polish her best silver spoons whenever I visited as a child.

Following Edward through the building, a woman stepped out of a storeroom with some bags tucked under an arm. They were the ones the customer's purchases went into so they could parade the name of the shop on their way home.

"Oh, hello," she said, recognising me from my many previous visits.

"Hi, Rhonda," I replied.

Mindy waved, and we waited so she could go ahead.

Edward led us to a room where two women worked. They were both bent over workbenches, large magnifying devices helping them to see the intricate work their hands performed. A wisp of smoke rose from one as she replaced what looked to me to be a soldering iron in its holster to her right.

They looked up as we entered, though only when each reached a point in their work where they felt they could afford to avert their eyes.

"This is Kitty and Alicia," Edward motioned to each woman in turn. "They are currently involved in checking and securing the mounts on several important pieces the King has commissioned as gifts for the Maharaja of Zangrabar."

"Oh, is that for his wedding?" asked Mindy, her question causing Edward to jolt.

He spun around to face my niece. "How could you possibly know about that? No one knows yet."

Mindy grinned and said, "When you know the right people ..." We knew about the young king's impending wedding only because we were with Patricia Fisher when her invitation arrived. Inside my head, I grumpily muttered that it was another royal wedding I wouldn't be invited to manage.

Suitably impressed, Edward waved for Kitty and Alicia to continue before leading us through the room to another door. This required yet another code to advance beyond and my brain was already questioning how a thief could possibly have defeated so many defensive barriers.

Passing through what I assumed was the final portal, I discovered another workshop much like the one we were just leaving.

"This is where the most valuable pieces are worked on," Edward explained once the door was closed to seal us inside. Mounted in a soft-jawed clamp on the desk was a tiara-style headpiece or crown from which was visibly absent a large jewel. Right in the middle of the piece a large hole sat between rows of symmetrical diamonds underneath which a row of smaller sapphires ran.

Mindy gave a low whistle. "You don't see those in the knock-off jewellery store in Rochester market."

She was undoubtedly right and for good reason. I couldn't put a price on the crown, but its value would run to millions.

Edward's voice cracked when he said, "It was there when I worked on it yesterday and it was only this morning that I noticed it was missing. Someone took the sapphire, and it can never be replaced. You have to help me get it back, Felicity!"

During the drive to London, I was determined to tell Edward I felt sympathy for his situation but that there was nothing I could do. I had the whole thing planned out in my head - what I would say, the tone I would employ, and how I would then help him to do the right thing and call the police.

Instead, I found myself now somehow telling him I would do my utmost to find the sapphire and bring the thief to justice.

Edward looked like he was going to fall to his knees and kiss my hands in thanks.

"You've no idea what this means to me, Felicity. To have a dear friend, someone I respect and admire, come to my aid in this way."

"Um, Auntie," Mindy nudged my arm with an elbow and hissed at me, "that's not what you said in the car."

How was I supposed to retract my statement now?

"Ah, you said on the phone that you think you know who has it?" I probed for detail.

Edward forgot his terrible anguish and got straight to the point.

"Yes, I'm rather afraid that I do and it's why I called you and not the police."

Good, he was going to explain why the authorities couldn't be involved and I longed to know the reason.

"Do you know the Duke of Westborough?" Edward asked in all seriousness.

"Not personally," I replied, having only the vaguest idea who that was. The name only rang a bell because his eldest son, the heir to the dukedom, died a few months ago in what the papers and news channels listed as mysterious circumstances. I knew nothing more than that, and couldn't pick the duke from a crowd.

Edward steepled his fingers in thought, before proceeding.

"I want to say that it brings me great pain to point the finger in this way, but it must be done. The duke's son, Lord Chamberlain, was here yesterday afternoon. He wanted to commission a piece of jewellery that he could wear to commemorate his brother's death. I'm sure you heard about it on the news. Terrible business," he remarked. "Edward is a member of the royal family and a permanent resident at Buckingham Palace. Such customers are treated differently because they are different."

I chose not to comment and cut my eyes at Mindy to make sure she wasn't going to say anything either.

"I don't often have customers in the back rooms, but as I said, a duke's heir and a member of the royal household warrants better treatment. However, I was called to the front desk during our meeting, so I left him perusing some designs I had put together."

"He took it while you were away," guessed Mindy.

Edward pursed his lips. "That is my assumption, but only because he was the only person back here. I was only gone for a short time and the door to my private workshop," he indicated where we stood to eliminate any ambiguity, "was locked. Only I know the code to open the door. It has been that way since I had the security door fitted. I cannot see how he got in and took the jewel, but there was no one else who had the opportunity to do so."

I swallowed, wondering what it was that Edward expected me to do. The son of a duke who lives in Buckingham Palace was accused of jewel theft. Did Edward really think I was going to be able to prove he did it and retrieve the jewel.

"You can help me, right?" Edward implored. "You've got that friend of yours ..." Edward looked away and clicked his fingers as if to jog his memory. "Victor? No, um, Vinny?"

"*Vince*," supplied Buster, wagging his tail.

"Vince," said Mindy, this time the name reached Edward's ears.

Edward snapped his fingers again. "That's it! Vincent. He's some kind of private investigator, isn't he?"

"Well, yes," I acknowledged, surprised that Edward would name a man he formerly considered to be a love rival. Edward hadn't spoken to me for weeks after the incident at dinner where Vincent, disguised as a waiter, interrupted our meal when Edward produced a ring box. When Edward did call, it was about business and nothing else with no mention of his previous desire to woo me. "He's a busy man though. I doubt he will be able to just drop what he is doing and come to help me."

Edward was distinctly more confident.

"Are you kidding, Felicity? I saw the way that man looked at you. He will reassign his work to one of his underlings and rush to your side. Together you will be able to solve my mystery, I'm certain."

From the floor, Buster's voice said, "*You don't 'need' Vince because you've got Devil Dog, but he's fun, so invite him anyway. I need to sniff around and find the culprit's scent. Can you lose Edward for a while?*"

"*Oh, for goodness sake,*" moaned Amber. "*Will you please stop pretending to have any idea what you are doing? If anyone is going to be able to figure out who did what here, it will be the cat. You're nothing but a fat, stupid dog.*"

Buster chose that moment to decide that enough was enough. He's surprisingly sensitive about his shape and likes to believe he is muscular and defined where in reality he looks like an overstuffed pillow with a face.

Launching himself at Amber, he did so by taking his lead the other way around my legs. Consequently, I was forced to spin or go airborne. I'm what most people would call petite and though I weigh more than Buster, his centre of gravity is roughly in line with my ankles. Consequently, when he decides he's going, he goes.

Mindy wasn't paying attention, and even with her ninja reflexes, Buster still caught her by surprise. It would help if she could hear my pets too, but since she can't she had no idea Buster was going to try to kill Amber until it was too late.

Jumping from the floor just as I lost grip of his lead, Buster slammed headfirst into the plastic cat carrier to knock it skyward.

Amber shrieked in fright, employing words that would make a sailor blush as she shot out of Mindy's hands and into the air.

Buster danced on his back paws, his mouth up like a hungry crocodile as he snapped his teeth in the air.

Mindy caught the carrier before it could land, but the jarring motion popped the door open, freeing Amber.

"*Dead meat!*" she squawked in that godawful sound only a cat can produce. Exploding from the carrier like Jackie Chan, she landed on Buster's face with all four paws. "*Move and I'll shred you like confetti,*" she threatened.

Buster, bright enough to recognise an untenable situation, froze.

"Now apologise," Amber demanded.

Speaking without moving his lips for Amber's claws were dug into the flesh above and below his mouth, Buster said, *"What for? You're the one throwing insults."*

"That's right. You are." I gripped hold of Amber by the loose skin and fur behind her neck. "Let go, Amber," I insisted.

"Not until he apologises for almost killing me."

"He did no such thing, Amber." I used my other hand to start prying her claws out of Buster's face one by one.

Mindy made an embarrassed noise above my head followed by, "Auntie does this. It's nothing to worry about."

Cringing, I realised that yet again I was talking to my cat and dog in front of someone and speaking to them as if I were able to hear their half of the conversation. It's not a gift, it's a curse.

When Amber's final paw came free, I tucked her under my arm and held her to my chest to make sure she was calm.

"I hate that dog," she said.

Leaning down to whisper into her fur, I argued, "No, you don't. You just don't know how to be nice to a dog and you worry other cats will find out if you are."

The look she gave me made me believe I'd just hit the nail on the head. Looking down at Buster to find him trying to lick the eighteen small holes his face now sported, I knew I needed to move the conversation along.

With a sigh, I faced Edward. "Look, I would love to help, but I really don't see how I can. Even with Vince involved, the person you suspect lives inside Buckingham Palace. It's not as though I can just go there and ask to see him. How am I supposed to investigate if I cannot ask any questions or do any snooping?"

Edward nodded in agreement, "Yes, yes, good point." His eyes were cast down, deep in thought.

Thinking he was coming to recognise there wasn't anything I could realistically do to better his predicament, I began to frame a sentence that would get him to call the police.

However, he snapped his fingers and looked up with a bright and hopeful expression.

"I know, I'll get you into the palace myself. It will be easy enough. I'm there all the time for one thing or another. It will have to be tomorrow though. Turning up this evening would raise a few eyebrows. How does that sound? Ready to solve a mystery?"

I didn't fight the deflated feeling or resist my shoulders when they drooped.

In complete contrast to how I felt, Mindy's voice came out with sparkles attached, "The palace? Really? You're going to get us into the palace? I have always wanted to take a selfie inside the palace!"

"Oh, um, sorry," said Edward, pulling an awkward face. "There are no cameras allowed inside the palace. Ergo, no phones."

"No phone?" Mindy breathed the words, too horrified by the concept to say them aloud.

"Don't you think you should call the police, Edward?" I tried to wriggle off the hook by making him see sense. "What will happen if I cannot find the sapphire or if Lord Chamberlain didn't take it?"

Edward's eyes flared. "But we can't call the police, don't you see? Not only would I be admitting to the world that my premises are not secure and thus eroding the faith that powerful families place in my establishment, much worse than that I would be pointing the finger at a member of the royal household. I would be ruined. No, I must gather the truth first. Only then can I expose it. That's why I need your help, Felicity. Yours and whatshisname."

"Vince," supplied Mindy.

Edward nodded. "Yes, Vincent." Seeing that I wasn't exactly committed to his cause, he pressed, "I wouldn't ask unless I were truly desperate, Felicity, and it will probably be an easy case to solve since we already know who is to blame."

"Please, Auntie," begged Mindy. "We get to go inside the palace."

I held up my hands in resignation.

"Okay, Edward. Okay. I'm really not sure what I will be able to achieve. I'm not a detective," I repeated a point I was fairly sure I'd already covered.

The crown-appointed jeweller thanked me profusely yet again, grabbing me for a quick hug even though I still held Amber.

When he released me just before Amber took a swipe at him, I said, "I need to poke around in here before I leave today, Edward. I will also need to speak with your staff and have a look at any CCTV footage you might have." Thinking on my feet, I added, "You can send that to me, actually." I didn't want to spend my evening in a back room of his shop when I could just as easily look at whatever film he had in the comfort of my own home with a glass of wine.

Edward spread his arms. "Feel free to look wherever you see fit. Open cupboards, check for fingerprints. Do whatever it is you usually do. I won't get in the way."

No, you won't, I thought to myself. Because I need you to leave.

"Can you get me that footage now?" I asked, holding out an arm to guide him back toward the door. "And figure out rough times for when Lord Chamberlain arrived and departed yesterday, please?"

"Oh, um, yes, of course." Edward left and I finally felt able to relax.

Mindy squealed with excitement the moment the door shut and we were alone.

"EEEEEEEEEeeeeeee! I wonder if we will see any of the royals. Do you think Charlie would pose for a selfie if I happened to, you know, bump into him? He'll have his phone, won't he? I could get him to send me a copy."

"Charlie? Are you referring to the King of England?"

"Yeah," Mindy grinned devilishly. "Charlie Boy the king. Do you think he would?"

"Pose for a selfie? No. He might send you to the tower for asking though."

Mindy made a grumpy face, but it didn't last; she was just too excited to go somewhere none of her friends ever would.

Placing Amber on the workbench, I turned my attention to Buster, and stroking his ego, I cupped his chin and said, "Now, I want Devil Dog, not Buster, is that understood?"

Buster's tail whipped back and forth until he remembered Devil Dog embraces the darkness and doesn't wag his tail.

"*Devil Dog is here,*" growled Buster in his Devil Dog voice. "*Who do you need me to neutralise?*"

"No one. I need you to sniff for clues. You've told me you can store scents in your head and find the person they belong to later."

"*I can.*"

"Then do that. Find the human scents in this room and elsewhere. When we go to the palace tomorrow," Mindy squealed again, "I will need you to find any scents that match the ones you find here. Can you do that?"

Buster lifted a paw to salute and almost fell over. Righting himself, he said, "*Affirmative.*"

Feeling that I was being quite clever for once, I let Buster off his lead and watched as he snuffled and snorted his way around the workshop.

Amber licked a paw and pointedly refused to pay him any attention. Thinking it might be best if I were to actually look around myself, I pulled open a few drawers just for the look of it and was sure to be looking intently at the tiara with the missing sapphire when Edward returned a few minutes later.

By then Buster had completed his sweep of the room and was ready to move on.

Edward had a data file – one of those little thumb drive thingies for me and a note to tell me what time Lord Chamberlain arrived and departed. He didn't want me to interview his staff yet; his mission to keep them in the dark dictating I couldn't quiz them on events regarding the tiara without tipping them off.

He did, however, answer a question himself.

It was the only one I'd thought of. "How could he have left the premises with the sapphire when you have so many security guards manning the exits. Why didn't it trip an alarm?"

"Well, there wouldn't be a tag on it, Felicity. Earrings, necklaces and such can be tagged so no one can run out with them, but the sapphire, while large, is still only the size of a golf ball. Lord Chamberlain could easily hide it about his person. It's not like my guards ask people to turn out their pockets."

So we left, piling back into the car to return to my cottage in Kent. It wasn't until I was about halfway home that I realised I didn't know when and how I was going to get into Buckingham Palace.

unexpecteD phone calls

I n the morning, eating muesli and running through a list of forth-
coming weddings in the peaceful quiet of my kitchen, I found myself questioning whether I ought to contact Vince. It was my practice
to not contact him, and the thought of reaching out sent a shiver down
my spine.

I knew what he wanted from me, and it made my stomach do flip flops
every time I gave it the slightest thought. There was no good reason
for my terror other than the simple fact that were I to venture into an
'actual' relationship with Mr Slater, it would be the first time since I
married Archie more than three decades ago.

If Archie was watching me from on high, he would most likely be
rolling his eyes now and reminding me he was long gone. He would

expect me to get on with my life, not act like it was over and bury myself in work – something I was constantly guilty of.

So I hadn't called Vince or messaged him – the traffic was all one way, and now I felt guilty that the first time I did reach out it would be to ask for his help which I knew he would gladly give.

Is life genuinely this complicated, or is it just me making it look that way?

Lost in thought, the abrupt chiming of my phone sent a stab of fear through my heart, jolting the muesli and milk laden spoon on its journey to my mouth. The spoon spilled, sending ice-cold liquid and breakfast grains down my pyjamas.

My brain insisted my thoughts of Vince had caused him to call, but the paranoia coursing through my veins proved wrong: the name displayed on my phone wasn't his. In fact, it wasn't anyone I expected to hear from.

At any point ever.

It was Primrose Green.

Primrose has a wedding planner business that she operates out of a plush office in West Malling. She is a former model and has the better of me by two decades, two cup sizes, and two kids. We ought to be friends – we have so much in common, but she employs dirty tactics to promote her firm as 'the' one to go to if one has money.

As such, we are rivals with a deep-rooted mutual dislike for each other. Why was she calling me early on a Saturday morning? I couldn't guess unless it was to gloat because *she* was awarded the contract for the impending and recently announced royal wedding of the King's third and youngest son, Prince Marcus.

I had allowed myself to believe I would come out on top in that particular fight, but I didn't, and the sting of my hubris lingered.

Forcing a calm breath, I picked up my phone and thumbed the green button to connect the call. Before I could say ... well, anything, though I had planned to lead with, 'Good morning,' Primrose was screaming obscenities in my ear.

"I know it was you! Don't bother trying to deny it! You miserable old cow!" Trust me when I say I have filtered out a whole bunch of expletives. "Only you would stoop so low. I knew you were jealous, but this enters a whole new realm. If you wanted a guerrilla war, well trust me, you've got one!"

The line went dead with my ears ringing and my brain struggling to join the dots. Mostly I was thinking, *'What just happened?'*. Primrose was about as upset as I had ever heard or possibly as upset as a person can be.

Why?

Good question. I had no idea. Staring at the phone with an accusing look – it spoiled the sanctity of my peaceful Saturday morning - I finished the last of my muesli and placed the bowl in the dishwasher.

SOMETHING STOLEN, SOMETHING BLUE

Was it going to ring again? Would Primrose calm down and call me back to explain her outburst. I thought the latter unlikely, but reaching to take it with me on my way back to my bedroom to get dressed, it rang again.

This time my fingers were just about to close around it and the sudden sound near gave me a coronary.

Snatching it up, I made sure to get in first this time.

"Primrose, I have no idea what is going on, but I do not appreciate being sworn at ..." The man at the other end cleared his throat with a polite cough. My response was so swift I failed to look at the screen to check it was her calling again. Gathering myself, I managed to say, "Um, sorry, I thought it was someone else calling. Good morning. How can I help you?"

Cursing, I wondered if the caller – it was only a number displayed on my screen – was a prospective client. What a way to leave a first impression. I dared to hope it wasn't someone really famous and waited for the man to speak.

"Good morning, Mrs Philips. This is Edgard Whitechapel."

Edgard Whitechapel? Why did I know that name?

"I am calling from Buckingham Palace on behalf of Prince Marcus and his fiancée Nora Morley."

My heart literally stopped beating and time stood still while I waited for him to say what I already knew he would. Primrose's call suddenly made sense.

"The wedding of Prince Marcus and Miss Morley is in need of a wedding planner following the ... untimely withdrawal of Mrs Green. Am I correct to assume you are willing to take the role?"

I breathed the word, "Yes," my brain giving me a mental slap and shouting that I needed to say it again, but audibly. Clearing my throat, I said, "Yes. Yes, please. It would be an honour."

Mr Whitechapel made a small noise of acknowledgement, and said, "Very good, Mrs Philips. You will need to attend a planning meeting with the Prince and Miss Morley at 1100hrs sharp today." There was no wiggle room, no question if that was convenient or messed with whatever else I might have planned. I was there or I was out; that was the message I got.

"Eleven o'clock at the palace," I repeated. "How do I ..."

"Be sure to bring photographic identification and bring your car to the North Gate on Constitution Hill. You will be expected. Do not arrive before 1030hrs. You may bring an assistant, but no cameras or phones will be allowed inside the palace."

Brain racing to keep up and process the information, I mumbled, "I understand. North Gate. Bring an assistant. Half past ten." Frantically, I looked about for a pen, but Edgard was already wrapping up the call.

"You will be expected, Mrs Philips. Please, do not be late. Good day." In the next second he was gone, his clipped upper-class accent replaced with the dial tone, and I was adrift on a surging current of emotions.

From a professional and personal point of view, the royal wedding was all I could ever ask for. Managing such an event would be the pinnacle of my career. Nothing would top this, but when it was awarded to Primrose a few weeks ago, I accepted the news with all the stoicism I could muster and tried to move on.

Oh, who am I kidding? I was heartbroken and had been doing my utmost to hide my feelings on the subject ever since.

Now, a change in circumstances caused a reverse in the palace's decision and the job was mine. Oh, my goodness, I had so much to do!

Reeling from the news, a worrying question slammed into me like a glass of ice-water down my back: had Edward done this?

Yesterday, he said he would arrange for me to visit the palace or have need to visit the palace; for the life of me I could not remember his exact words now. Overnight, Primrose had lost her coveted spot at the top of the heap so I could replace her.

No wonder she was spitting mad: she thought I did it.

A crunch of gravel outside my kitchen window and a shadow drew my eye to see Mindy returning from a run. It was cold out and she wore a fitted black top that came down to her hands and thin gloves to stop her fingers going numb. She had ear buds in and I caught the tinny sound of music when she popped them out coming through the door.

She was a little out of breath and condensing water vapour rose from her shoulders and head until she shut the door to seal the cold air outside.

"Morning?" she said, cautiously examining my face. "Is everything okay? You look like you woke up next to a body." She turned her back on me to open the fridge, closing it a moment later with a carton of almond chocolate milk in her hand. Drinking from it, she faced me again.

"We have the royal wedding," I announced plainly.

Mindy chugged some more chocolate milk before saying, "Huh?"

I didn't feel that my statement required much explaining. Nevertheless, I said, "The royal wedding. The one due to take place between Prince Marcus and Nora Morley. The one which was awarded to Primrose Green. That is now ours, or mine, I should probably say. I got a call from the palace while you were out running."

Mindy's face bore a confused look.

"How did that happen? Did Primrose drop out? Is she dead?"

I released a deep sigh. "She is most definitely not dead; I got a call from her about two minutes before the palace called. She is rather upset and whatever it is that happened, she is blaming me for it."

"But you've got the contract to arrange the royal wedding. How much is that worth?"

I would find out in more definite terms later today, but I knew what I bid for it and Mindy's eyes almost popped out when I told her.

"Oh. My. God, Auntie. That's insane!"

"It's not going to be easy, and we are behind the curve because it went to Primrose first. We've lost weeks."

Mindy finished the milk and dropped the carton in the bin. Settling onto a stool at the breakfast bar, she dug her phone from a hip pocket and began to tap on it, both thumbs flashing across the screen at a speed it seemed only young people can achieve.

I was thinking about how to say I thought Edward might be behind the shift at the palace when her mouth dropped open and she uttered an expletive.

Before I could chastise her, she turned the phone around to face me and I used the same word.

The single picture displayed told me everything I needed to know, but the headline was the clincher.

'ROYAL WEDDING PLANNER IN SOFTCORE PORN SCANDAL'

Certain areas of the picture were blurred out. Specifically where the detail was not the sort of thing a news outlet can display. Not even an online one. Reaching across, I used a finger to scroll because there were more pictures, a whole photoshoot of them.

Primrose had a career as a model when she was young and the pictures were clearly from her late teens or early twenties. I thought she did mostly catwalk and glossy magazines and had no idea she stooped even so low as glamour let alone what I was seeing now.

"Oh, that poor woman." The words slipped from my mouth as the full horror of her situation dawned on me. I believe most people have that dream where they find themselves naked at work and wake to find themselves safe in bed to their enormous relief.

Well this was so much worse than that. She ran a business and no one there would look at her the same now this was public. She had a husband and children too. The kids were young and could probably be shielded from the scandal, but had her husband even known the pictures existed?

Losing the contract for the royal wedding would come as a harsh blow, but the fallout would go so much further.

She might have done it to herself, but we all make rash decisions as we go through life. She might have been coerced into the photoshoot or too young to know better. Maybe she needed the money. I could not imagine a circumstance where I would have resorted to such a strategy, but that didn't mean I was prepared to condemn her for something she might have spent her life wishing had never happened.

Mindy cocked an eyebrow. "Poor woman? She hates you. She's a loathsome, venomous snake who recently tried to scare you from your boutique by faking that it was haunted. Should you not be rejoicing?"

I sighed again. Could I rejoice? I mean, I was over the moon that I had the contract for the royal wedding, a contract I had always felt ought to be mine anyway, but I couldn't be happy for the way it came about.

Without warning, Mindy gasped. When I turned to look at her, my niece's eyes were aimed right at me and the size of goldfish bowls.

"Auntie did you do it?"

"What? No!"

"Really," she asked, not believing me. "Because, you know, eliminating the competition like that would be a seriously slick move."

I was horrified she could think I was capable of such a thing.

"Mindy, I can assure you, not only would I never do such a thing to any woman, even if I wanted to, I had no idea these photographs existed."

Flicking my eyes to look at the clock, I announced that I was getting dressed and told Mindy she had less than an hour to get ready. Traffic would be slow this morning; weekends always are, even in the capital, but there was still no time to waste if we were to arrive on time.

Hurrying to my bedroom, I returned to my question about Edward: was this down to him? How did he come by the photographs if it *was* him? He and I were old friends, but I knew he could be as ruthless a businessman as anyone else when he needed to be - few firms thrive without someone strong-willed at the helm.

My thoughts of Edward naturally reminded me that he expected me to somehow find the time to snoop when I was at the palace. Would he be meeting me there? Dare I ask if he scuppered Primrose?

All in all it felt like I had fallen through the looking glass and my heartrate was high because I suspected the worst was yet to come.

HOW TO CLAIM A PALACE
AS YOUR OWN

I almost took Archie's Vintage Ford Mexico again, but how could I drive that up to the palace gates and expect to be taken seriously? Sure I had to take Buster and Amber with me and had no idea how that was going to go down, and they didn't exactly fit in my two-seater sports car, but I wasn't seeing a third choice.

"We could take my car, Auntie," Mindy pointed out.

Mindy drives a Renault Clio Williams Supersport which is a car designed to go extremely fast in an urban setting. A boy-racers car. The sort of car a hooligan drives on their way to sell drugs. I might be stereotyping a little, but much like the vintage Ford, it was hardly the car the woman running the royal wedding should arrive in.

Actually, what I ought to arrive in is a Bentley being driven by a chauffeur in a suit and hat. Since I did not have one of those to hand, the only option left was my Mercedes SL into which the four of us crammed.

To be fair, Amber's kitty carrier went behind my seat where there is always a gap because at five feet and five inches, I am forced to pull the seat all the way forward just to reach the pedals. In the passenger seat, Mindy pressed her legs to one side which allowed enough room for Buster though the daft dog kept trying to get on her lap where he claimed he would be much more comfortable and would be able to see out of the windows.

"*I'll get car sick down here,*" he whined.

From behind me, Amber's voice taunted, "*I thought superheroes were too badass to get sick.*"

Mercifully, Buster wasn't sick and fell asleep before I reached the motorway.

I called Edward once we were settled into the drive.

"Felicity, good morning. I was just about to call you. I spoke with Sir Cuthbert, the Master of the Palace this morning, whereupon I discovered you were being appointed as the wedding planner for Prince Marcus. Congratulations, my dear!"

If he was behind Primrose's fall from grace, he was doing a good job of hiding it. I chose to leave it for now and he got in first anyway.

"I wonder what happened to make Primrose withdraw."

"Oh, um, I couldn't guess," I mumbled, not happy to lie, but unwilling to bring up the truth of it. Edward would find out soon enough, but not from me.

"Well, I was going to ask if you could meet me there; I told Sir Cuthbert I had some of the late Queen's pieces to return, which is true, and that I would be bringing an assistant – you. Am I right to assume you will be attending the palace today anyway?"

"Yes. I have an appointment with the Prince and Miss Morley at eleven o'clock. Will I see you there?" Was there now an opportunity to weasel my way out of my promise to snoop? It's not like I wasn't going to be busy today and for the foreseeable future.

"Oh, indeed, my dear. I will look out for you. Once you are finished with the future bride and groom, I can help you to access the right places. It's surprising how a little familiarity allows me to go where others cannot."

Hanging my head in acceptance – I just wasn't getting out of the investigation, I was hit from left field when Edward asked his next question.

"Do you have Mr Slater with you?"

I'd completely forgotten to call him! Fear of the task kept me awake last night and woke me early this morning. Whether that was through concern for how he would behave or a refusal to acknowledge my own feelings when it came to the man with the shark-infested smile, I was yet to determine.

I had been on the cusp of placing the call when Primrose rang. Since then, Vince hadn't once crossed my mind.

"Oh," replied Edward, disappointed by my news. "Well, perhaps you can conduct some preliminary investigation and get him to meet you there later today. You have every reason to visit the palace now and I was able to confirm the young Lord Chamberlain is currently in residence."

The call ended with yet another iteration of my promise to do what I could to find the jewel and save Edward.

Approaching the palace, I drove slowly. There wasn't much traffic around, but I still got a few horn toots while I stared at the palace and tried to figure out where to go. Thankfully, the gate was right where Mr Whitechapel said it would be and relief that I had arrived a few minutes early replaced the worry I might get there late.

Mindy squealed again as I pulled up the barrier. "This is so cool!"

The armed police officers, not soldiers as some people seem to think – the army are just there for decoration at the front of the palace – checked my ID and logged my visit, recording my face and Mindy's using a little camera on a stick.

Permitted entry only because we were expected, I was given an assigned parking space and met at the car by a woman in a suit carrying a radio in her left hand. She wore a deep blue winter coat that fell to her thighs and fitted black trousers above short-heeled black ankle boots. Her coat was open to show a pale blue shirt beneath, also fitted, and had her ash-blonde hair cut into a bob that met her jawline.

She looked all business and introduced herself as Detective Inspector Munroe.

"Mrs Philips?" she enquired, though I felt certain she already knew who I was from her radio. She shook my hand and then Mindy's too. "You brought your dog?" she asked, surprised to find Buster at Mindy's feet.

A touch of heat came to my cheeks. I'm a professional wedding planner catering to the rich and famous and I do not visit their houses for meetings with my cat and dog in tow. I wouldn't have them here either were it not for Edward's pleading. Not that he knew I was going to attempt to use Amber and Buster to expose the truth.

Trying to act as though this was all normal, I said, "And my cat too. I go everywhere with them." Perhaps if I played the diva card, I would fit right in.

DI Munroe seemed to consider it for a moment, but with a slight shrug, she turned back toward the palace. "Follow me, please."

She was forced to wait while Mindy and I unloaded brochures, my laptop, and some other paraphernalia from the boot of my car. It was cumbersome to say the least and I hoped we were not going to have to carry it too far.

The grounds of the palace were immaculate as one might imagine they would be. On the short walk to the nearest door, I saw not one cigarette butt or discarded piece of litter. It was as if the wind knew better than to blow rubbish in off the streets.

Inside the palace, things were no different, which is to say I was in the most spectacular and opulent residence I had ever seen. The television fails to do it justice and we were not even in the residential areas yet.

"Please don't touch anything," DI Munroe warned when Mindy stopped to look at a bronze bust.

For a moment I thought the detective was going to escort us all the way to our destination, which seemed wrong, but was not the case. She merely took us inside the building through what I guess would be referred to as a tradesman's entrance and to a reception area where a senior member of staff looked over the top of his reading glasses at me.

"Sir Cuthbert, this is Mrs Philips and her assistant," DI Munroe announced.

The name was the one Edward used – the Master of the Palace. Sir Cuthbert was in his late sixties, or a little older but looking younger. He bore a stern expression though I took it to be his resting face. A shade under six feet, he wore a tweed suit with a waistcoat and pocket watch I was willing to bet was bought by his great grandfather more than a century ago. His tie was that of the Queen's Regiment. Though now disbanded, or perhaps the right word is amalgamated, into several other regiments as the need for a large standing army reduced, I knew of it because the Queen's Infantry were local to me in Kent and some of the boys I went to school with had joined them.

Sir Cuthbert was opening his mouth to address me when Buster sniffed the air noisily, drawing attention to himself. I thought for a moment I was about to have a problem, but the Master of the Palace cracked a wide grin.

"What a handsome fellow you are," he said, rounding his desk to meet my bulldog. Halfway there, he dismissed DI Munroe, "Thank you Detective Inspector, unless there is something else?" His tone wasn't exactly unfriendly, but there was no warmth to it either.

I caught DI Munroe's eye, and she gave me a quick nod before turning away without another word.

When Sir Cuthbert lowered himself to fuss Buster, I took the opportunity to unburden myself of the heavy brochures I carried, dumping them on Sir Cuthbert's desk.

Sir Cuthbert was down on one knee, fussing Buster who flipped willingly on his back to have his tummy tickled.

From the cat carrier, Amber remarked, "*Oh, so ferocious. Look at the idiot with his tongue hanging over his eye.*"

Looking up at me, Sir Cuthbert said, "I have one myself at home. I've always had bulldogs, in fact." He gave Buster one last scratch under his chin and rose to his feet. "My mother used to breed them. Now then, Mrs Philips and Miss Walters …"

"Mindy," said Mindy.

Sir Cuthbert eyed her sceptically. "Pleased to meet you, Miss Walters," he made it clear we were on formal terms. Turning his attention back to me, he returned behind his desk. "Here to see Prince Marcus and the bride-to-be." Reaching to his right, he lifted a small silver bell which he rung before putting it down again.

Buster said, "*I like him. He smells like bacon.*" He nudged my leg. "*Ask him if he's got any.*"

A man in what I assumed to be official palace livery appeared a heart-beat after the sound of the bell died away.

"Carrow, please escort Mrs Philips and Miss Walters to the Oxford Library. Prince Marcus and Miss Morley will meet them there. Bring tea for four."

Carrow, who looked to be in his mid-twenties and skinny as a rake which wasn't helped by being well over six feet tall, dipped his head in greeting and begged that we follow him. Gathering the brochures, though I insisted he wasn't to attempt to carry them all, he set off.

Our route through the palace to that point had all been along the ground floor, level with where we parked the car. I thought the décor and surroundings were plush, but discovered that was because I hadn't seen what the rest of the palace looked like. Turning the next corner, I got the full effect.

The corridor or hallway along which we walked was wider than my living room is long and the walls stretched a mile to the ceiling far above our heads. Like everything else, the carpet, the paint, and all the bits in between were immaculate. Where the ceiling met the walls, ornate fancy bits – I'm sure they have a name, but I didn't know what it was – bled one into the other and what looked to be gold and probably was adorned the pattern to make sure everyone saw it.

Mindy's eyes were like saucers, and I suspected mine were too. The palace was an interior designer's dream come true.

Buster said, "*This place is nice. We should move in.*"

A snort of amusement left my nose, causing Carrow to turn to see if I was attempting to attract his attention.

"It's not much farther," he let us know.

I didn't care if it was. The more of the palace I got to see the better. I couldn't very well respond to Buster and thankfully he understood that.

"*I tell you what. I'll just claim it for us,*" he remarked happily.

My wide eyes widened a good deal further when my brain translated his statement, and I whipped around to yank on his lead before the bulldog could lift his leg against a wall.

"No, Buster! Naughty!"

"*But how am I supposed to make this place ours if I don't leave my mark everywhere. I just need to pee in every room ... that might take a while, but when I have, this place is ours, lady. I bet I can do some amazing power skids in these corridors. I wonder if they have any without carpet.*"

53

I can do them on carpet if I get enough speed, but my nipples get sore if I do too many."

I tugged his lead again, pulling him tight to my side and with my eyes boring into the top of his skull insisted, "No peeing in the palace, Buster."

With a jerk, he twisted his rugby ball shaped head around to stare at me with a deeply quizzical expression.

"That's just crazy talk."

"No peeing," I hissed insistently with Carrow craning his head around to see what was happening.

Buster fell into silence (if one ignores the constant snuffling noise he makes when he breathes) and I returned to drinking in the incredible architecture and decoration. But not for long. Remembering I was supposed to be finding and snooping on Lord Chamberlain for Edward, though the very concept made my blood run cold, I wondered how I might ascertain where to find him.

I could hardly ask which room was his. Ironically enough, I didn't have to.

Entering the corridor ahead of us came a handsome man in his late twenties. Dressed for polo and with a thick coat slung over one shoulder, I think he heard when Mindy muttered, "Hubba, hubba," a little louder than she should.

Certainly a broad smile split his face and Mindy's cheeks flushed bright red.

"Good morning, ladies," he hallooed, continuing to close the distance between us.

"Good morning," I replied, panicking because I didn't know whether to address him as 'Your Highness', 'Your Majesty', 'Sir', or something else. Was he a member of the royal family or something else entirely?

Mindy mumbled her own greeting just as Carrow said, "Good morning, Lord Chamberlain," with a slight bow of his head."

Startled to find I was looking at the very man Edward believed to be guilty of stealing a priceless sapphire, I also found it difficult to correlate the possibility of crime with the striking image before me. Of course, I now recognised him from Edward's CCTV footage I half-watched last night. Annoyed that I felt obligated to view it, I did so with a glass of wine in my hand and one eye on a re-run of Downton Abbey. Consequently I paid very little attention, but the man before me was the same one from the footage, so Edward wasn't lying when he said Lord Chamberlain was at his shop. Maybe he was right and the royal was a thief.

Carrow got a "Good morning" in reply, though Lord Chamberlain's eyes lingered on his for no more than a moment before returning to Mindy.

"You have the advantage of me," he said, the smile still in place though it now possessed a slight wolfishness.

Mindy, her cheeks still glowing, said, "Um, what?"

"Well, you know who I am, though I suppose a less formal greeting is in order. My name is Eddie."

As if in a trance, Mindy repeated, "Eddie."

"Yes," Lord Chamberlain smiled, "Eddie. My father is the one who gets called 'sir' all the time. He's the duke."

"Your father is a duke?" asked Mindy, sounding more and more out of place all the time.

I wanted to come to her rescue, thank Lord Chamberlain, and hurry her along, but the fact that he was now chatting with us gave me an opportunity. I could strike up a conversation, ask him questions. Maybe say that I was a friend of Edward Smallbridge and see how the young lord reacted. Would I see guilt in his eyes? That was something Patricia Fisher often talked about; being able to tell if people were guilty.

There was no chance to do anything yet though, not without rudely interrupting. I wouldn't say I was happy to have him flirting with my niece, since that is what he was clearly doing, but as suitors go, provided he wasn't also some kind of gentleman thief, I could hardly pick someone better.

Eddie, as we were apparently now calling him, turned himself to face the way we had been going.

"How about I walk with you. What are these ladies here for, Carrow?"

"This is Mrs Philips and Miss Walters, sir. Mrs Philips is taking over the wedding planner role for Prince Marcus and Miss Morley."

"Oh?" He cocked an eyebrow. "I wasn't aware there had been a change."

I thought for a second he was going to ask what might have caused such a switch, but the subject held no interest. Unlike my niece.

"So, Miss Walters, finally I have a name, but to address you in such a manner sounds rather pompous and formal for two such attractive, young people."

He was asking for her first name but doing so in such a roundabout way poor Mindy failed to follow him.

With bewilderment in her eyes, she mumbled, "Huh?"

This drew a guffaw from the lord.

"I'm sorry, my dear, you must forgive me. I was enquiring as to your first name. May I address you informally?"

Mindy swung her head around to stare at me, a little panic showing in her eyes. Looking back at Eddie a heartbeat later, she said, "Huh?"

Beginning to worry he might assume she suffered from a mental capacity issue and give up, I prompted her.

"Your name, Mindy. The gentleman was asking for your name."

"Indeed," laughed Eddie. "Though doing a spectacularly bad job of it." Thrusting out his right hand for her to shake, he said, "Pleased to meet you, Mindy."

Buster asked, "*Are they going to mate now?*"

It was a good thing Mindy couldn't hear my dog's voice; she was already embarrassed enough.

Amber replied, "*No, humans are waaay too complicated to just get on with it. They have all manner of daft rituals to go through and can take days, weeks, or even months to get to the mating part. It's so bizarre. Find a mate. Do the mating. Walk away.*"

One of the hardest parts of being able to hear my pets' thoughts and words was resisting the need to react as though everyone else could hear the same thing.

Mindy had shaken Eddie's hand and looked to have relaxed a little. He was pointing out some of the palace features and regaling us with stories about living here as a little boy. Mindy was staring at his shapely bottom clad in tight jodhpurs and doing little to hide her obvious interest.

When she felt my frown, she looked my way to mouth, "Oh. My. God!" followed by miming grabbing a handful of butt and biting it.

I got what she was saying but wasn't about to approve or endorse her opinion. Instead I changed my frown to a glare - we were here to work. Although, I had to admit Mindy was unexpectedly in a position to leverage answers we might otherwise be unable to get.

Thinking fast, I was about to interject in their conversation when Carrow spoke.

"Here we are."

He stopped outside the open door, beyond which lay a huge library. Clearly waiting for us to enter, I turned to see what Lord Chamberlain would do.

Raising his muscular right forearm to check his watch, he grimaced and swore.

"I really must dash. The chaps get so upset when one of us is late and it's generally me." Reaching out to take Mindy's hand again, he lifted it to his lips as he bowed his head. "I do hope I will get to see you again. Perhaps, since I must abandon you at this juncture, I could be thoroughly forward and give you my number?"

He let the question linger in the air for a second, holding Mindy's gaze.

I caught Carrow's eye and nodded that we should go through the door. Right now.

Catching my drift, he scurried through the door before I felt the need to hook his arm and take him. Buster trundled ahead, happily sniffing and snorting the air. He'd said nothing about Lord Chamberlain's scent which I believed he would have if it matched what he smelled in Edward's workshop the previous day.

The library walls were lined with thousands upon thousands of books. Tables and chairs and other options such as a pair of plush chaise longues provided places where a person could sit if they planned to remain in the library to read.

However, Carrow led me to a pair of sofas arranged around a small coffee table where he placed my heavy collection of brochures and we waited for Mindy.

"Does Lord Chamberlain have a history of flirting with young women visiting the palace?" I enquired.

Carrow's voice was utterly devoid of emotion when he said, "I couldn't possibly comment, Mrs Philips."

Mindy came through the door, looking around to spot me a few seconds later and had the decency to look embarrassed. Carrow, of course, said nothing, acting as though the incident either wasn't worth mentioning or had, in fact, never happened.

When Mindy arrived, Carrow took Amber's cat carrier from her, placing it carefully on the carpet next to the low table.

"Please make yourself comfortable." He waited until we were seated before asking, "Is this your first time meeting a member of the royal family?"

"Goodness, yes," said Mindy with a nervous laugh. "Well, except for Eddie." Her cheeks coloured again under my glare. "I mean Lord Chamberlain." She placed a hand on her forehead as though feeling her temperature and flapped her hands in front of her face. "Is it hot in here?"

I had never seen her this on-edge before. Even when we are being chased by someone with a gun she rarely acts as if she is scared or anxious. Today she seemed all sixes and sevens.

More calmly, I replied, "No. Not my first time. We need to address the prince as 'Your Royal Highness' upon first meeting him," I guessed why the young man had raised the question. "Thereafter it is 'Sir'. Got that, Mindy?"

Mindy nodded, but said, "Do I curtsy?"

Carrow shook his head. "Not for such an informal occasion. Please address Miss Morley as 'Miss Morley' unless invited to do otherwise. No matter what, do not feel tempted to address Prince Marcus by his first name."

Suitably advised, Carrow dipped his head and turned toward the door. I stopped him with a question.

"Where is the nearest restroom, please?"

"Just along the hallway on the right," Carrow indicated which way to go.

I let Carrow depart, waited until he was out of earshot, and hit Mindy with an amused look.

"Get his phone number, did you?" I teased. "The phone number of the man we came here to spy on?"

Mindy's grin held no shame. "The number of the superhot son of a duke. Did you see his bum? He can't be behind the missing jewel, Auntie, he's gorgeous!"

The sound of footsteps, quiet on the carpet outside, halted our conversation, but it wasn't the prince and Miss Morley arriving but Carrow returning with a tray of tea. He brought the silver platter to our table and withdrew, advising the tea required time to steep and he would return to serve momentarily.

The happy couple would be along soon enough and when we were done discussing wedding plans, I imagined we would be escorted from the premises. Thinking I might have to concoct a clever ruse to get out of the room to investigate a little further, Buster provided a way to do that without employing my imagination.

"*I need to go outside*," he announced. "*It's poo time.*"

"I don't need the details, Buster," I sighed.

"What's he saying?" asked Mindy.

"That he needs to go outside."

"*Because I need to poo*," explained Buster unnecessarily. It wasn't as if Mindy could understand him.

"Can you take him?" I asked, knowing she would. The prince and Miss Morley could arrive at any moment, so it wasn't as though I could go.

Mindy took his lead. "Come on, Buster. Let's see if we can find our way out of this maze."

"*Yay! Poo time!*" he barked happily, somehow finding joy in everything.

From her carrier, Amber said, "*I've said it so many times in the past, Felicity: you need to get rid of that awful creature. What madness inhabits your mind to keep him around I cannot conceive, but if you cannot bear to part with him, I'm sure we can find a good taxidermist.*"

Tutting, I opened the door on her carrier. There was no sound from the hallway outside, and I figured I could get her out for a brief cuddle.

I was wrong.

Treacherous cat

Whether they wore shoes that made no sound, or were secretly ninjas, the bride and groom snuck up on me without a sound.

I recognised them both, of course, their faces had been in the papers ever since Miss Morley came on the scene. The country was hungry for another royal wedding and with his two elder brothers already married and producing kids, Marcus was the last prince worthy of such attention.

With the official announcement of their engagement just a week ago, there wasn't a news outlet failing to cover the story. It helped that Miss Morley was particularly photogenic. High cheek bones set beneath dark brown hair and eyes the colour of chocolate complimented a perfect smile and a figure most women would kill for.

She had brains too, her career as a lawyer dictating she came into the relationship as something close to an equal partner. In fact, if one were to remove the family money, she would be the breadwinner.

"Goodness!" I exclaimed, juggling Amber. "So sorry, Your Majesty. I didn't hear you coming." I was trying to reverse my grip on Amber, who complained about me insisting she go back in the carrier, when the prince surprised me.

"Oh, look at that beautiful cat, Nora!" He left her side, dropping his grip on her hand as he came forward to get a closer look. "Is it … is she a Ragdoll?"

"*You have a good eye,*" said Amber. "*And you are observant too; I am beautiful.*"

"Yes, Your Majesty," I replied, still flustered. "She is a ragdoll. This is Amber."

Miss Morley asked, "Darling how did you know it was a girl?"

He smiled lopsidedly. "It's in the shape of the face and the eyes. Girls are more delicate and pretty."

Amber dug her claws into my hands where I held her.

"*Hand me to him. I want to be fussed by someone who truly appreciates me and doesn't think making me share a home with a flatulent, slobbering dog is a good idea.*"

Wincing, I fought to control her as she tried to get free.

"Can I hold her?" the prince asked, holding out his hands.

"*Yes, you may!*" grunted Amber, digging her claws in a little further and struggling against my grip. "*Hand me to the nice prince, Felicity. Your services are no longer required. I shall live here with him instead.*"

With no say in the matter, I passed her into his arms. Amber would shred my hands if I failed to comply, and telling the prince no so I could stuff my unruly cat into her carrier would just be rude.

"Oh, my, aren't you a sweet little kitty?" Prince Marcus cooed. "I've always wanted a house full of cats. They are such majestic creatures."

Amber climbed the prince, her little claws tearing at the fabric of his shirt though he seemed not to care. Arriving at face level, she proceeded to scent rub herself all over his skin.

There were a lot of words I wanted to say to my cat at that point, and were I not in Buckingham Palace in the company of actual royalty, I might have said them rather loudly.

Biting my tongue as my cat whored herself for the prince (yes, I used that word about my own cat, treacherous moggy that she is), I asked, "Shall we get down to business?"

Nora, for one, looked pleased to be able to start the meeting, though Prince Marcus continued to coo at Amber. The couple sat opposite me, their faces expectant.

"Let me start by thanking you for selecting me to help you plan your wedding. It is a rare honour to be granted such a prestigious opportunity."

The prince waved me to silence.

"You come highly recommended, Mrs Philips, may I call you Felicity? I believe we will be seeing a lot of each other over the coming months."

"Of course, sir," I replied, half expecting him to reciprocate by inviting me to call him Marcus.

Mercifully, he did not, but Nora jumped in with, "You must call me, Nora. I beg you. My life is about to change so dramatically, I fear these next few months are the last time I will hear people other than family using my first name. It takes some getting used to."

Prince Marcus settled Amber into his lap and took hold of his fiancée's hand; giving her something to cling to perhaps in the maelstrom of change she currently endured.

"The truth, Felicity," said the prince, "is that you were our first choice for the event."

This came as news to me.

"We were overruled, you see," he continued to explain. "We wanted a wedding planner who was local to the event."

"And that narrowed the field considerably," Nora picked up where her intended left off. "It was your run of recent bad luck that spooked some of the household's advisers."

"We're not saying Mrs Green was a disappointment," said the prince, picking his words carefully, "but in light of recent revelations," he chose not to expand on what that meant and undoubtedly trusted that I would already know of the breaking story, "we were forced to switch and that gave us the chance to put our feet down, so to speak."

Whether it was the absolute truth or not didn't matter. Primrose was out and I had the job now.

Opening my notebook, I clicked my pen and asked, "Do you have much of the wedding already planned?"

PICK YOUR SPOT

M indy had to go looking for a way out of the palace; that was problem number one. Her bigger concern, however, was that Buster was going to poop on the royal lawn. The palace and its grounds were utterly immaculate. What was she supposed to do about a steaming pile of poop? She didn't even have a baggy with which to scoop it. Why would she? Buster isn't her dog.

Hopelessly lost but spotting another young man in the same palace livery Carrow wore, she called to get his attention.

"Hey, hello."

The young man turned slowly, his arms full of silverware he looked about ready to drop.

"Oh, goodness. Would you like a hand with that?" she offered.

Buster huffed, "*I really don't think this is going to wait, Mindy.*"

Had she been able to understand the dog, she might have reacted, but to her it was just doggy noises.

The young man looked about nervously to see if anyone else was about before saying, "Do you mind? I'm seriously worried I might drop something, and Sir Cuthbert will probably sack me if I do."

Looking at the silverware and then at her hands, Mindy offered Buster his own lead to carry.

"Here, bite that, Devil Dog, and keep up. I'm sure this won't take a moment."

Buster raised one eyebrow but opened his mouth to take the leather lead.

"I'm Mindy," said Mindy.

"Heathcote," the young man replied. He had a touch of acne around his jaw and looked to be about her age Mindy judged, wondering how a person got a job at the palace.

"That's not your first name, surely," she challenged, taking a silver platter from the top of the pile and unhooking two jugs. The rest of it chose to shift, threatening to cascade to the floor until Mindy closed the gap to support it with her body.

Unfortunately, Heathcote tried to save the load himself, raising the hand now less encumbered by the two jugs and in so doing grabbed a handful of something at chest height. Mindy's chest height to be precise.

Bright as a beetroot, Heathcote began to apologise.

Mindy laughed at him. It had been a complete accident.

"Now I can honestly brag I got groped in Buckingham Palace." His face went a shade darker. "I might choose to be a little fuzzy about who the perpetrator was though," she chuckled. "Come on, where is this lot supposed to be going?"

Cheeks still burning, Heathcote mumbled, "To the silver room. Quite why we have to take them elsewhere to clean them, I have no idea. It's just down here."

Unnoticed by Mindy, Buster left a mark on the wall where they had been, happily trotting along behind them with one small portion of the palace claimed.

The silver room matched the name – floor to ceiling shelves of silver-ware in a windowless box.

"Just put it anywhere, thank you," Heathcote dumped the items he carried carefully onto a table. "Next time, I'll make two trips. Is there anything I can help you with?"

Mindy wanted directions to the garden, but got a guided tour through the catacomb of corridors in the palace's lower levels instead. Fetching up at a door that led outside, Mindy remembered the other thing she needed.

"Um, Buster here ..."

"I thought you called him Devil Dog earlier? Now that *is* a cool name."

"I know, right!" snorted Buster. *"Devil Dog is my alter ego and a name not to be spoken by just anyone. In truth I ought to use my mind powers to erase your memory, but I really need to go for a poo so it will have to wait."*

Heathcote stared down at the dog. "Did it sound like he was trying to tell us something?"

Chuckling to cover her terror and yet again wishing she had her auntie's gift, Mindy said, "Don't be silly. He just needs to go outside. I wouldn't want him to have an accident inside the palace."

"Perish the thought," Heathcote agreed.

"I could do with a baggie. Something I can use to pick up after him. Also," Mindy added, thinking fast, "is there somewhere people take their dogs? I mean the Queen had all those corgis, they must have needed to poop somewhere."

Heathcote opened the door and took her outside where he pointed to a path leading into the gardens.

"There's a favoured spot just down there on the right where it is out of sight from most people. Take him there and I'll fetch a plastic bag you can use."

Buster was already tugging at his lead. *"This isn't going to wait much longer!"*

Mindy jogged, allowing Buster to run like the fat, furry missile he is. Under the trees and out of sight, just as Heathcote said they would be, she cautiously unclipped his lead from his collar.

"Pick your spot, dog. Just don't wander off."

The sensible thing was to keep him on the lead, but that meant standing inside a tiny circle of disgusting stench and Mindy would rather risk having to chase the daft mutt around the palace grounds than breathe in what he was putting out.

"*Pick your spot, pick your spot,*" muttered Buster. "*You humans have no idea the science that goes into such a simple instruction. This is a complex task that requires careful consideration of multiple factors: grass length, the presence of spikey or stingy weeds, air flow direction ... Hold on, here it comes anyway.*"

Mindy moved away, wrinkling her nose and trying not to breathe as like her mum she questioned what her aunt might have been feeding the dog.

Through the trees she could see Heathcote returning, but blinking when something else caught her eye, Mindy stared at the undeniably gorgeous shape of Lord Chamberlain as he slipped back into the palace through a back door.

He'd changed clothes and was moving with the mid-morning shadows, or so it seemed. No longer in the tight-fitting jodhpurs, the shape of his pert behind was now hidden inside loose-fitting black cargo trousers.

Were royals allowed to wear cargo trousers? Mindy had no idea if the highest members of British society had dress regulations or not, but he looked wrong in them regardless.

More importantly, he was back in the palace when he was supposed to be somewhere else playing polo. Did this mean he had lied to her? Or was polo unexpectedly cancelled? Maybe his horse needed a shoe? Was that a thing? Mindy lived in the city and had never been on a horse unless the donkeys at Margate beach counted.

Curious and questioning what she could do to find out if perhaps he really was guilty of stealing a priceless sapphire, Mindy jumped clean out of her skin when Heathcote spoke just behind her head.

"I have the bag," he announced.

Thankful for good bladder control, Mindy had to take a deep breath and laugh at herself to hide her embarrassment. People were not supposed to be able to sneak up on her. She spent years of her life training for it to be the other way around.

Recovering from the shock, Mindy noted that not only did Heathcote have the bag, the man had already collected Buster's offering.

"You didn't have to pick up after him," Mindy said, thoroughly happy that he had.

"It seemed the least I could do, after ..." his eyes flicked down to her boobs and realising what he'd just done, Heathcote's head turned scarlet again.

Mindy might have told him to stop worrying but her brain overruled her mouth. There was a massive discrepancy from the current picture.

Frantically looking around for Buster, Mindy's heart sunk. "My aunt is going to kill me."

BUSTER'S NOSE

B uster thought about waiting for Mindy but caught Lord Chamberlain's scent on the air and assumed, since she was staring at him, that she planned to get on with mating. He could find his own way back to Felicity, not least because he'd left several marks along the way.

Besides, left to his own devices, he could probably leave his scent all over the palace and claim it as their new home. It sounded like a good plan and then there was the other thing he was supposed to be doing, Devil Dog's voice echoed in Buster's head to remind him: track down the jewel thief.

It was a task for a superhero and no mistake, but he was confused about who he was supposed to be investigating. There were several human scents in Edward's workshop yesterday, but none of them belonged to the man who wanted to mate with Mindy.

At least, Buster didn't think they did. The workshop had stunk of metal polish and other harsh chemicals which threw his nose for a loop. Also, he knew humans could disguise their smell and his nose wasn't the best in the canine world.

It was a design thing, you see? Pugs had it even worse, but like them his nose was too short and snotty to be efficient or effective. He'd never let Amber know it. However, though he believed Lord Chamberlain had never been inside the workshop where the jewel went missing, he couldn't be one hundred percent sure.

Regardless, Felicity made it clear she needed his help for this particular task, and he was going to provide it.

Pausing to listen at the palace door when he thought for a moment he'd heard Mindy calling him, Buster witnessed Felicity's niece taking off in a different direction. Little did he know she'd just seen another dog in the distance and assumed it was him.

With the canine equivalent of a shrug, he nudged the door open with his face and squeezed inside.

WHERE'S BUSTER

With Heathcote in tow, the young man still carrying the bag of poop, Mindy shouted for Buster to slow down and tore across the palace gardens to intercept her aunt's stupid dog. Taking a jog through the palace gardens was a great adventure and all – she would have stopped to take selfies if she was allowed to bring her phone, but fear she would be spotted and chased by security or the army or something was making her heart pound.

Where the heck was Buster?

Coming around a large wall of shrubs, she spotted a dog, but it wasn't the one she wanted. It was a corgi. In fact, it was several corgis.

They were being managed by two young women in the same palace livery Heathcote wore, albeit tailored to their female form.

Nearest to her, a redhead said, "Good morning, ma'am," and looked across to her colleague, a brunette, who dipped her head and said the same thing. They were immaculate, just like everything else at the palace, and had their hair pulled into matching tidy French plaits.

Guessing they were about her age, Mindy was about to reply when Heathcote got in first.

"Hey, girls," he puffed, a little out of breath from chasing after Mindy. "Have either of you seen a bulldog in the last few minutes?"

"A bulldog?" repeated the redhead.

"Yes, sorry. He's mine," Mindy admitted. "I'm Mindy. You don't need to call me 'ma'am'. I took my eyes off him when he was pooping, and he vanished. I thought I saw him over here, but now I worry I saw one of these dogs. Are they the Queen's?" With the Queen gone, what were the dogs still doing here?

The redhead nodded. "They are. When she passed so suddenly, her dogs were brought back here. They will live out their lives at the palace. Your bulldog didn't come this way, though, sorry."

Groaning her annoyance, Mindy puffed out her cheeks and looked around. Should she shout for him? Was that allowed at Buckingham Palace?

Naughty Cat

"So, you see, Felicity, the structure of the wedding and its skeleton, if you will, are already in place. Money has changed hands and all that we now require is for you to take the baton." Prince Marcus finished explaining and turned to his fiancée to make sure there was nothing he'd missed.

"If you are willing, that is," added Nora, her voice hopeful as if I might turn down the prestigious contract.

With a smile that hid my fluttering heart, I took a breath so as not to snap their arms off, and said, "Yes. Thank you for inviting me here to review your wedding plans. It would give me great pleasure to ensure your marriage gets off to the perfect start."

The prince leaned forward in his seat. "And there's nothing here that seems daunting or too complex? We are dealing with far more guests than the average wedding and many of them have important political ties to our nation. The importance of ensuring they are all correctly catered to cannot be overstated."

The truth was that while he was not wrong, this was far from the biggest or most complex wedding I had ever been asked to manage. Nor was the guest list particularly daunting. Unable to figure out how I might express that without coming off as overconfident or boastful, I chose to say, "My team is experienced and well trained, sir. I need a little time to process the guestlist, but I wish to assure you both that your nuptials could not be in safer hands."

They looked inward at each other, the happy couple holding hands and chatting about minor details and the family pressure to get it all right. Left out of the conversation for a few moments, I reviewed their plans.

Most of it was run of the mill for me and made vastly easier than usual because Primrose had already laid the bulk of the ground work. Whatever else I wanted to say about the woman, I could not deny that was she a highly capable wedding planner.

Amber was asleep on the prince's lap, a contented purr rising from her as though she were powered by a small motor. She cracked one eye when I glared at her, snapping it shut the moment she saw me looking. The dirty little faker was just pretending to be asleep.

The time was heading toward noon and my stomach felt decidedly empty – the muesli hadn't done the trick. My business would be concluded when the prince and Miss Morley said it was, but I could feel they were about ready to leave.

A knock at the door drew the eyes of everyone in the room.

At the door, Carrow bowed his head respectfully.

"Sir, please excuse this intrusion. I have a message for Mrs Philips."

Prince Marcus let go Nora's hand and shuffled his bottom to the edge of the seat to get up.

"Come on in, Carrow. We were just leaving. Unless you've anything further for us today?" he left the question hanging to see if I would need to delay them leaving.

I rose to my feet. "No, sir. Thank you both once again. I have everything I need for now." I wouldn't be dealing with the prince and his intended directly from this point forwards – there was a palace appointed liaison instead. I guess they don't like giving out the royal family's phone numbers. If I needed to ask them a direct question, it would be arranged through the liaison person.

Nora got to her feet, but Prince Marcus was having a touch of difficulty.

With my cat.

"*No! No! I don't want you to put me down!*" wailed Amber. "*Take me with you and let me live here! This place is much more in keeping with my station in life.*" She was digging her claws into his trousers and probably his flesh if the wincing noises the prince made were anything to go by. Latched onto his thighs, he was standing upright and she still wasn't letting go.

"Ah, is there a trick to this?" he asked me, trying to make light of the situation though I was utterly mortified.

Carrow crossed the room, delivering a folded piece of thick white paper on a silver tray.

"For you, Mrs Philips." He dipped his head when I took it and withdrew, undoubtedly hoping to escape before he was collared into helping to save the prince from my insane feline.

"Amber, let go now, please," I demanded in a stern voice.

She dug her claws in further, eliciting fresh wincing from her victim.

"No. I'm not going with you. You make me live with a dog!"

Had she been clinging to his chest or an arm, I would have grabbed her, removing her by force and prising her paws off one by one if she refused to yield. However, with my cat clinging like a limpet to the prince's groin, I couldn't figure out where I could possibly place my hands.

My temperature rising in line with my embarrassment, I ummed and aahed, continuing to berate Amber who hissed at me when I came near.

"Go away! I'm all fine here. I know you'll miss me, but it's your own fault for having the dog. If you had just had him stuffed like I suggested, we wouldn't be in this situation now."

Nora bent at the waist, trying to take hold of Amber though she continued to make low growling sounds of warning. Each time she

83

unhooked a paw, the prince now biting down on a knuckle and staring at the ceiling to find a happy place, Amber simply took a fresh grip the moment Nora moved to the next leg.

"Felicity, I think perhaps what we should do is come at her from both sides. If we take two paws each ..." the prince's bride-to-be suggested.

We both got on our knees – not the most lady like position ever, and gripped the cat.

Amber twisted her head to lock eyes with me.

"You're going to ruin this for me, aren't you?"

Unable to answer her question directly, I narrowed my eyes and said, "Amber you are a very naughty cat." I brought her to the palace so she could help me with Edward's delicate problem. Her involvement, however, was looking thoroughly unlikely now.

Amber's threatening growls grew in volume as Nora and I carefully removed her paws one by one. Just as she was about to come free, I heard someone come into the room behind us.

I twisted my head to find Mindy in the doorway, her mouth open and her eyes popping from her head.

"Wow," she murmured, beginning to back away when what I needed was for her to come and help.

Suddenly I realised how it must have looked from her perspective – two women kneeling on the carpet in front of the prince with their heads at his waist height. Tearing Amber free, I jumped to my feet, but I was too hasty and lost my grip when my cat chose to fight again.

Flying through the air, Amber twisted her body around to make sure she landed on her feet, she yelled, "*I'm not going back to live with that awful dog!*" She bounced off the couch, her legs already powering her across the room toward Mindy.

My niece had a hand to her chest and a show of immense relief on her face now that she could see what had been going on, but recovering from her shock, she was too slow to intercept my speeding cat.

With a final meow of, "*Goodbye, my prince!*" she hurtled past Mindy's feet, made a hard left turn and vanished from view.

"Um, everything all right?" asked Mindy. "Wedding plans all sorted?" she saw my expression and pointed the way Amber had just gone. "I should try to stop her, right?" She didn't wait for an answer, bolting from sight just like my cat.

It was only after she was no longer in view that a question forced its way to the front of the queue: Where's Buster?

Superhero Work

O nce Buster was inside, he found himself with an entire palace to explore. There were humans around, but they were easy to avoid.

Ordinarily, when marking a new territory, he would go into every room and leave his scent behind. Today the sheer vastness of the palace was defeating him.

"*I need to refuel*," he muttered to himself. His last attempt at cocking his leg had produced nothing but mist. It was perhaps the fiftieth such mark in the palace and he was coming to the realisation that an entire pack couldn't hope to leave their scent everywhere.

Without water to replenish his reserves, it was going to be a while before he could renew staking his claim, so with Devil Dog's reminders echoing in his brain, he set off to find the person behind the jewel theft.

Yet again, the vastness of the palace proved problematic. He had the scents from Edward's workshop locked in his brain, but finding a trace of them here was going to be difficult. Pushing on even though his paws were getting tired and he fancied a nap, Buster clung to the belief that he was the only one who could help Felicity in her time of need.

It wasn't as if the cat would do it. So far as he was concerned, Amber was the spawn of hell just like every other cat he ever met.

No, it was down to him. So whether his nose was a bit rubbish compared with other dogs or not, he was going to keep going until he found the jewel thief.

Some minutes later, having lumbered up a flight of stairs and ducked down a passageway when he heard someone coming, Buster's nose did indeed catch a scent he recognised.

It wasn't one he could associate with any he found in Edward's workshop. Equally, it wasn't one he could ignore either.

SPYING

My niece returned a little more than a minute later. She was out of breath and her clothes were rumpled from running. More pertinently, she was neither carrying nor accompanied by Amber.

"I can't find her, Auntie. I can keep looking, but I didn't want to just wander the palace. What if I bump into the king?"

"I thought you were going to get a selfie if that happened," I remarked uncharitably. Hearing how unfair that sounded once the words were in the air, I apologised. "Sorry, Mindy. This isn't your fault."

"Where's the prince?" she asked. "I didn't even get to meet him."

"Applying salve to his ... legs," I chose to say, not entirely certain Amber's claws hadn't found some more, ahem, *delicate* spots. "There will be other chances for you to meet royalty, Mindy. Lots of them, I believe."

"The wedding contract is all sorted then?"

I nodded thoughtfully. "Yes." It was. The royal wedding, a thing I had coveted since it first became a possibility, was mine to manage. If one could claim a pinnacle in one's professional life, then this was it for me.

"What do we do about Amber?"

I was tempted to say something along the lines of, "I can get another cat," but even though she had a terrible attitude and acted as though she hated living with me and Buster, I knew that wasn't the truth.

Before answering, I looked down at the note in my hand. It was from Edward. Having no phone certainly changed how a person could communicate. I understood the royal family's need for privacy and that mobile phones provided a full suite of video recording apps. It was still strange to not have it in my possession though.

"Amber will have to wait," I announced, gathering my brochures and getting Mindy to help. "Edward is downstairs somewhere and has asked that I join him. I expect he wants to know if I have found his jewel thief yet."

Mindy asked, "Shouldn't we wait for Carrow?"

The answer, of course, was a resounding 'yes' but if we did that the chance to snoop would be lost. He was taking the tray of tea to wherever that went, and I was going to do what it would never occur to me to do under any other circumstances – I was going to sneak around Buckingham Palace and spy on people.

Encumbered by the weight of my brochures which showed cakes, wedding dress styles, flower displays and much more, I struggled back into the hallway.

Knowing we would need to stop for directions, I deliberately set off in the wrong direction, not because I wanted to explore, which I did, but because Lord Chamberlain had come from this way. Would we find his rooms if we looked around a bit? It wouldn't be hard to claim we were lost; I felt certain it was a daily occurrence for any guests left unattended as we were.

Giving Carrow the slip before he could return, I set off at a brisk pace.

"Keep your eyes peeled, Mindy. Not just for Amber and Buster," I was struggling to believe I'd lost both pets at the same time, "but for Lord Chamberlain's rooms."

"You mean Eddie?" she smirked, teasing me with her 'first name terms'.

Giving her my most disapproving frown, which seemed to just bounce off her perky attitude, I said, "No, I mean Lord Chamberlain. Please try to remember we are employees here." The correct term was 'contractors' but that was just splitting hairs. "I know he's handsome, Mindy, but getting involved would be a mistake."

Mindy stopped walking.

When I turned to look at her, she had a frown on her face.

"Why? Because I'm not good enough for him? You think he'll use me up and discard me? I'm not a child, Auntie."

She was angry; an emotion I'd never seen on her face before.

"That is not what I said."

"It sounded a lot like it," she snapped. Starting to walk again, she passed me, speaking at me rather than to me. "You sounded just like my mum."

Her unexpected reaction caught me off guard. I was trying to look out for her, and truthfully, I did suspect the rich, handsome member of the royal family would happily have his way with my niece and cast her aside for the next filly to meet his gaze. I could be wrong, but he seemed the sort and hadn't it been that way with men of power since the dawn of time?

My right foot twitched as I started to go after her. I needed to reel her in – she was my assistant after all, but I also needed to calm her down and make it clear I was on her side – us women have to club together. However, from the corner of my eye, through the window as I passed it, I spotted the very man Edward accused of theft.

"Mindy!" I hissed after her. "Mindy!"

"What is it, auntie?" she replied impatiently.

I stole a quick glance in her direction to make sure she wasn't still walking away, and looked back through the window.

Lord Chamberlain said he was off to play polo, but little more than an hour had passed since I last saw him. Was it right that he was back in the palace already?

Mindy meandered back to where I was standing.

"What are you looking at?" she asked, picking the next window to look through. She squinted but saw nothing because Eddie, as Mindy liked to call him, had walked out of sight.

"It's Lord Chamberlain," I whispered. "I think that's his room." I meant rooms, of course. The building folded around a courtyard where I was standing, and though I tried to orientate myself, I couldn't figure out where I was in relation to the front of the palace.

Regardless, I was looking across the courtyard at a forty-five-degree angle when the man in his polo shirt reappeared. There was a lot of palace; was it all accommodation? I guessed a lot of it had to be so they could host dignitaries and royalty from other nations – who wouldn't want to spend the night at Buckingham Palace?

"He said he was going to polo practice," I accused with a whisper.

Mindy nodded. Our disagreement over the man forgotten for now, she said, "I don't think he had time to leave the palace grounds. I saw him heading back into the palace when I was trying to find Buster."

Right before my eyes, Lord Chamberlain stripped off his polo shirt to reveal a lean, muscular torso beneath.

Mindy growled like a happy tiger getting ready to pounce on its next meal. Unlike me, she didn't turn away, but chose to continue watching.

"I know I said it before, Auntie, but that man is too gorgeous to be guilty. Although he ought to be charged with something," she added, "because he has got 'fine' written all over him."

I rolled my eyes. "Well, now we know where his rooms are, we can deploy my special weapons to look for the missing sapphire."

Knowing I was referring to Amber and Buster, Mindy turned to meet my eyes. "We could if we knew where they were."

Just then Carrow came running around the corner, a worried look plastered to his face and a sense of desperate relief that he'd found us.

"Mrs Philips! Thank goodness. I've been looking all over. I'm afraid there's been a small incident."

I closed my eyes and prayed this wasn't about Buster.

Carrow sucked in some air – it sounded as though he'd been running for some time. "It's your dog, I'm afraid."

used and Betrayed

We found Buster with Sir Cuthbert and, to my surprise, Edward. We were not where we met the Master of the Palace, but in what proved to be his private office. The air contained a distinct aroma of bacon which demanded explanation, but would have to wait.

"Edward," I greeted my old friend as I came into the room. He crossed the floor to meet me, touching arms when he leaned in to press his cheek lightly against mine in an air kiss.

"Felicity." Whispering through my hair, he asked, "Have you found anything?"

I pulled back to look into his eyes as we broke apart. Was he seriously asking me to tell him now in front of Sir Cuthbert? Was the Master of the Palace in the know?

Edward gave a slight shake of his head and lifted a finger to his lips. Facing away from Sir Cuthbert, the gesture went unseen, but my confusion persisted.

Buster was bustling around my legs, jumping up and wagging his tail so hard his back legs were leaving the ground. Rather than appear sheepish or ashamed, my bulldog's face possessed a contented expression.

Sir Cuthbert rose to his feet.

"Mrs Philips, I have to report that Buster broke into my office and stole my lunch – a bacon sandwich with HP sauce." He described the sandwich as though it were nectar from the gods.

"*That's right,*" grinned Buster, looking up at me.

"Oh." The bacon smell was no longer a mystery at least.

"Yes," agreed Sir Cuthbert. "Oh, indeed."

Mortified yet again – what was it with my pets today? – I did my best to apologise.

"I'm afraid he got away from me outside," I admitted, leaving out the part where it wasn't me at all.

Mindy jumped in to defend me. "It wasn't auntie. Please don't think bad of her. I took him outside to poop and he ran away."

Sir Cuthbert almost spat out his teeth. "You took him outside to poop? In the palace gardens? Is it still there?"

Mindy said, "Of course not," giving me some sense of relief. "Heathcote found me a bag and he took care of it."

Sir Cuthbert rubbed his forehead.

I was getting ready to apologise yet again and wondering how to break the news about Amber being loose somewhere in the Palace when Edward stepped in.

"Come along, Sir Cuthbert, Felicity isn't the first person to visit the palace with her pets. Nor is she the first to lose one." Chuckling, he said, "Remember the ostrich ..." He couldn't continue because he was laughing too hard.

I had no idea what he was talking about, but Sir Cuthbert clearly did for he was laughing too. In an instant, the rather stern man went from stressed to amused.

"I thought we would never get the stains out," he barely managed to burble around his laughter, the pair of them clearly reminiscing about an incident in the distant past.

Snatching a breath, Edward made a squawking noise that made them both double over. When their hilarity subsided more than a minute later, Sir Cuthbert was no longer upset about Buster and the missing bacon sandwich.

"Well, I guess there's no good crying over spilt milk," he sat back down into his chair and rubbed Buster's ears and scalp. "If you were any other breed ... well," Sir Cuthbert looked up to meet my eyes, "I trust your meeting with Prince Marcus and Miss Morley went well."

"Yes, thank you."

Coming from somewhere in the distance outside Sir Cuthbert's office, a cry of outrage over a mark on the wall triggered an alarm at the back of my head.

Flaring my eyes at Mindy, I sent her to get Buster and said, "I really must be getting along, actually, Sir Cuthbert. Unless you have anything further for me …" When he didn't respond immediately, I said, "Yes, really must be going. So much to do and such a compressed time frame. Picking up after someone else to plan a wedding is so much more work than one might imagine," I lied, ushering Mindy to the d oor.

"There's another one!" The complaints echoing down the hallways outside were getting louder and coming closer.

Edward's face revealed his confusion. "Felicity? Um, are you leaving?" He thought we ought to be doing something else, but I was done. For now at least. There could be more adventures at the palace later, but I wasn't about to investigate Lord Chamberlain or anyone else right now.

"Walk with me," I invited, waving a goodbye to Sir Cuthbert as I hurried out the door and away from the approaching drama I felt certain had everything to do with my dog.

With Edward hurrying to catch up, I hissed at Buster, "Did you piddle all around the palace?"

"*No!*" he exclaimed, much to my surprise. "*I ran out five minutes into the job. We own a couple of corridors but I'm going to need help to claim the rest of it.*"

A muscle by my left eye twitched. More commonly that happened when I was being troubled by Vince. Just ahead of me, with Mindy leading him to the exit, Buster's derriere presented a very kickable target. I resisted, obviously, but I won't say the thought never crossed my mind.

Outside in the cool winter air, I made a beeline for my car.

Mindy stopped halfway there, a thought causing her feet to stop moving, "Auntie, what about Amber?"

"Stuff her!" I shot back. Then I too stopped and a tear slipped out to run down my left cheek before I could swipe it away. "She said she didn't want to live with me any longer and ran away. She wants to live with Prince Marcus."

Buster whooped, "*Hooray! That's amazing! I thought we would never be rid of her.*"

Seeing red I snarled, "This is all your fault, Buster. If you were nicer to her, she might still be with me!"

Scared, Buster took a step back.

"The pair of you are as bad as each other. Why can't you just get along and be nice? Is that too much to ask?" I was close to a full-scale blub now, my eyes feeling too big for their sockets, and I needed to blow my nose.

Edward caught up finally. "I see you were unable to get Mr Slater to join you today …" He stopped talking when he saw my face.

I wasn't expecting it, but he pulled me into his arms, wrapping me in his embrace.

"Oh, my poor, sweet, Felicity. Have I asked too much of you? I am such a fool." He kissed the top of my head, which was a little weird and he was definitely holding me for longer than was generally acceptable for two persons not in a relationship.

I separated myself carefully, easing back so we stood two feet apart and I was closer to Mindy than I was to him.

"I'm afraid today has been rather trying, Edward. I need to leave now." *Before the palace staff catch up to me and have Buster stuffed and planted in the garden as a warning to other dog owners.* However, seeing Edward's pained expression and remembering how distressed he was yesterday, I had to give him something. "I promise to return. I was able to identify Lord Chamberlain's private rooms and will reveal his behaviour today was suspicious."

Mindy tutted. "All he did was come back early from polo practice, Auntie. It's hardly a crime."

"We can discuss it on the way home," I offered, not wanting to get into it here.

"You will involve Mr Slater, won't you," Edward got in quick. It was the fourth or fifth time he'd pushed to have Vince involved and it finally dawned on me it was my connection to the private investigator/security specialist that drew Edward to contact me, not my supposed sleuthing skills.

Feeling a little used, and possibly a tad betrayed, Edward disarmed me with his final words.

"The entire future of my business is in your hands, Felicity."

I slid into the car and out of sight with Mindy and Buster just as a woman in a suit stormed out through the same exit we used. She looked mad and I wasn't hanging around to find out for sure if she was after Buster and his owner.

Driving home, I almost missed the exit to get off the motorway. I was so wrapped up in my thoughts it took a nudge from Mindy to remind me where we were.

Amber was missing and my heart felt heavy for her absence. Sure, she's a grumpy, ill-mannered, treacherous thing, but that's pretty much the same as calling her a cat. She was my cat and she loved me really.

Didn't she?

Edward was another problem I could not seem to escape. Why had I not put my foot down yesterday and refused to get involved? I knew the answer: I never could refuse a friend in need. I would call Vince and do what I could, but was I really going to go back to the palace with him to snoop on a member of the royal family? Could I be that reckless? What if I got caught? Could I somehow explain away my actions?

I sighed, unable to find answers to any of my own questions.

On top of it all sat the royal wedding. I ought to be over the moon. Today ought to be the best day of my life, yet somehow I felt sick with worry. In recent months, pretty much every wedding I organised suffered problems. There had been murders, dresses had been stolen, cakes were destroyed, couples realised they didn't even care for each other on the eve of their nuptials ... the list went on. That these weddings were for celebrity couples in the most part ensured they made the news and each time that happened it felt like another nail in the coffin of my career.

What if this one went south too? What if something happened to a member of the royal family? No one would blame me; that would come down to the police and security forces drafted in to protect the royalty and dignitaries attending.

Yet there would be guilt by association. No one would convince me otherwise.

I didn't know it yet, but my worst fears were going to come to life far sooner than I thought.

Home Truths

G inny started to complain the moment we walked through the door.

"Where have you been all day? I was bored. Neither of you took your phones with you. Was that just so you could ignore me like my husband?"

Mindy chose to deal with her mother, and I let her.

"Mum, we were not allowed to take our phones. We were in Buckingham Palace, and they were very clear about their policy. And dad is not ignoring you. He's waiting for you to apologise and show that you want to be married to him."

"Well, he might as well wait for hell to freeze over," she snapped in reply. "I haven't done anything wrong."

"So you keep saying, mum," Mindy sighed while walking away. She was unwilling to give her mother relationship counselling and who could blame her? They say divorces are always hardest on the kids and I was thankful my niece was an adult. Even so, I could see her parents breaking up was affecting her. Was that behind her outburst earlier? She almost bit my head off when I questioned Lord Chamberlain's motives.

Taking a moment to consider it, and assuming he wasn't behind Edward's missing jewel, I was probably wrong to suggest he would discard her the moment he got what he wanted. I had no evidence on which to base such a claim.

I would talk to her about it later. Not now though because Ginny was coming my way.

"I suppose you think I should apologise too," she snarled coming into the kitchen. "Play the role of the weak woman and let him dictate how I live."

Opening the fridge, I took out a bottle of wine. That Ginny hadn't drunk it all while I was out came as something of a shock until I realised it wasn't the same one that was in there this morning.

Pouring myself a generous glass, I scooped it up and turned to face my sister.

"Don't worry," she sniped, "I'll get my own."

She reached up to get a glass from a cupboard but turned around to find the wine bottle was back in the fridge and that I was blocking her access to it.

"Ginny, you should apologise to your husband." She was instantly trying to shout me down and I had to fight to get in first. "Which has nothing to do with being weak or allowing him to dictate your life. Even if you get a divorce, you should apologise because you are in the wrong. Apologising would be the strong thing to do and might go some way to creating parity in your relationship."

Behind Ginny, Mindy came to stand quietly in the doorway.

"Don't talk about divorce. We are not getting a divorce." Ginny said the words, but her voice was quiet for once and just a little afraid. Also, there was no conviction in her statement.

"You will if you refuse to talk to him and it must start with an apology. Shane has always provided for you, and what do you give him in return?"

"Love," Ginny stated firmly.

Mindy snorted and left the room before her mother could spin around to see her.

"What was that, young lady? What did you mean by that noise?"

Her voice echoing from the hallway beyond, Mindy said, "I'm not a child, mother, so I don't act like one. Maybe you shouldn't either."

I could see Ginny was going to blow a gasket. She had never been the most reasonable woman and now she was getting verbally beaten up by everyone around her. That she would assume a defensive posture was only natural.

"Please, Ginny," I begged. "Look at our situation as an example."

Her face set into a hard mask of pain and denial, she looked down at me. "What situation are you talking about? Do you mean me begging a space in your house and you doing almost nothing to make me feel welcome?"

I nodded, the gesture one of acceptance for it was a typical Ginny response.

Trying something new, I said, "From my perspective, my sister appeared on my doorstep one day with her bags and her daughter expecting to be let in. You didn't ask if it was convenient ..."

"I'm your sister," she pointed out as though that was explanation enough.

"Yes, and I would have given you a place to stay no matter what. However, it is also accurate to say you are my sister who hasn't bothered to visit or call me in a decade. A sister who doesn't even send me birthday or Christmas cards, and a sister who has yet to think it necessary to thank me for putting a roof over her head. You are not nice to me Ginny and I believe you treat your husband much the same way – as a person who is there to be at your beck and call as and when you need them."

"A fair-weather friend," said Mindy, back in the doorway again. "Aunt Felicity is right, mum. You might not like it, but I spend more time with dad than you do."

"He's always burying himself in his work," Ginny argued. "He's never home for me to spend time with."

"That's because you don't bother with him when he is around." Coming from her daughter, Ginny was unable to fight back with claims Mindy would instantly dismiss as false. "When did you last go out to dinner with him? When did the two of you last sit together and watch the sunset while drinking a bottle of wine. You used to do that all the time when I was little. I would play in the garden and my parents would watch. I don't want you to get a divorce and I am here with you instead of at home with dad, but I won't pretend anymore, mum. You make my dad unhappy, and I love him too much to defend you."

It was quite the statement. For a moment I thought Ginny was going to turn volcanic, reacting to our unwelcome truths by throwing insults, curses, and her version of the truth. She did none of that. Instead, she began to cry.

Not just tears and weeping, but full uncontrollable sobs that wracked her body. One moment she was stock still in the middle of my kitchen, the next she looked ready to collapse.

Mindy ran to her, keeping her upright as they held each other.

I downed my wine and poured another.

WHO'S AT THE DOOR?

F eeling awkward in my own house and wanting an excuse to lock myself away, I ran myself a bath. Buster had taken himself into the living room where he sprawled across the couch content there was no cat to share it with.

Seeing him made me sad all over again. Leaving in such a hurry, I failed to even report we left Amber behind. With a jolt I remembered the cat carrier. It didn't come with us so must have been left in the Oxford Library. No doubt a servant found it, but if there were questions about my cat, they were yet to find their way to me.

I soaked in the hot water for most of an hour, a slight buzz from the wine sending me into an almost comatose state of relaxation, but worry for my cat refused to dissipate. Chances are, I told myself, Amber was cuddled up on Prince Marcus's lap right now.

I was being silly though. Much as the prince thought she was beautiful, he wasn't going to keep her just because she chose him over me.

Shortly before deciding I had soaked for quite long enough, Mindy knocked on the bathroom door and called through it to ask if I wanted pizza. It was late and dinner hadn't happened. Typically I would make myself a roast on a Saturday, even when it was just me. That required a trip to the supermarket though, plus thought and preparation. None of those things happened, so pizza would have to suffice.

Dressed and getting hungry, I found Mindy in the living room fiddling with her phone. Ginny was nowhere in sight which I presumed to mean she was in her bedroom locked away thinking about her options.

"Mum went to see dad," Mindy announced without looking up. "She got all dressed up for it. I think she might actually say something sensible to him."

I wanted to shout 'Halleluiah!' but restrained myself. Instead I voiced my hope that they could work their way through things.

My bottom was just settling into my favourite position on the couch when the doorbell rang. Mindy bounced out of her chair, moving far faster than I could.

"Pizza! Pizza, pizza, pizza!" she cheered, racing to the door.

I flicked on the television, thinking I might watch it while I ate. There was much I needed to do not just for the royal wedding but for others I had taken on. My diary doesn't fill like many wedding planners who have at least an event a week for much of the year. Aiming for a higher class of clientele, I rarely average more than one a month. This is because the big events demand a long run up and ... well, let's just say I get twitchy if I do nothing for too long.

Mindy was taking longer than the transaction ought to require, a sentiment echoed by my stomach which grumbled like a flatulent walrus. Listening for her return, I could hear her talking to someone. No, it was more than one voice, it was two. Plus Mindy's.

Then the front door closed and the talking continued.

"Auntie," Mindy said as she came back into the living room with guests.

Thankful I chose to put clothes on instead of just my pjs and a robe, I stood to greet the people coming through the door and was surprised to find I recognised them both.

One was DI Munroe and for a heartbeat I wondered if she was returning Amber. There was no sign of my cat though.

The other person was a woman too, although on closer inspection, not that I was about to say anything, she had several manly features: big hands, an Adam's apple, and what looked like a trace of stubble coming through on her chin.

I knew her face, but could not for the life of me place where from.

"Mrs Philips," DI Munroe addressed me. "I hope you can excuse this invasion of your home. We," she indicated the blonde woman to her left, "have a rather delicate matter to discuss with you."

"Am I in trouble?" I asked, trying to keep the nervousness from my voice.

DI Munroe hitched an eyebrow. Looking at her colleague as if for guidance, she looked back at me. "Not that I know of. Can we sit?"

The doorbell rang again, Mindy dashing off to get it once more.

Indicating the chairs I made a point of speaking to the other woman.

"Have we met?"

"Jane Butterworth," she shook my hand. "I work with Tempest Michaels at the Blue Moon Investigations Agency. We didn't exactly meet, but I was in the office when you came in."

I could picture it now. She was in the back talking to someone else; another client perhaps when I visited their premises.

Reversing back into my spot, I asked, "So what brings you here?"

They didn't get to answer straight away because Mindy arrived with two boxes of pizza. "It was only a quid for the large instead of the medium. We'll never eat it all so if you ladies are hungry, please dive in." She placed the boxes on the coffee table and ran back to the kitchen for plates and napkins.

The ladies were hungry, but tucking into their slices of pizza, they got to the point of their visit.

"You met Lord Chamberlain today, yes?" DI Munroe wanted me to confirm though I felt sure she already knew the answer. When I did, she said, "What I am about to tell you cannot be repeated outside of this house."

Wondering what she was going to tell me, I mumbled, "Okay," around my mouthful of pizza.

DI Munroe looked for Mindy to consent also.

Mindy chewed fast so she could swallow., but instead of agreeing she asked, "Is this going to be about something being stolen?"

Jane and DI Munroe checked with each other, their questioning faces leaving no doubt they had no idea what Mindy was talking about.

Seeing that, Mindy was quick to say, "Obviously not. Forget I said anything. Please continue. Oh, and yes, I acknowledge that I'm not allowed to tell anyone whatever it is you are about to tell me." She mimed crossing her heart.

DI Munroe's eyebrows did a little dance until I said, "She's nineteen."

Choosing to press on, Munroe said, "We have reason to suspect Lord Chamberlain was involved in his brother's death." It was a bold statement.

Munching more pizza, Mindy said, "Auntie's friend thinks he stole a sapphire."

I flared my eyes at her. "That's supposed to remain a secret, Mindy."

She made an 'oops' face. "Only joking?" she tried weakly.

DI Munroe looked in my direction for a better explanation.

Sighing, I said, "Look, I don't know that Lord Chamberlain has done anything. However, Mindy is not wrong; a friend of mine claims a priceless sapphire went missing and that Lord Chamberlain was the only one around at the time."

"You're talking about Edward Smallbridge, yes?" The police officer demonstrated how much she knew. "Hold on!" her eyes widened. "Priceless sapphire? Are we talking about the Heart of Windsor?"

Oh, dear Lord. Edward didn't want anyone to know, least of all the police and I'd just let the cat right out of the bag.

Backpeddling as fast as I could, I said, "There is no actionable information to follow up and Edward begged me to not tell anyone. He intends to figure this out for himself."

DI Munroe raised an eyebrow. "I think I might need to have a word with Mr Smallbridge. The longer he leaves it, the colder the trail will go. The crime may have happened outside of the palace, but the jewel belongs to the royal family and that makes it part of my remit."

I massaged my temples and did my best to drown out the voices in my head. I told Edward I wasn't a sleuth. I can't even manage to keep a secret. Hoping to move to a different subject, I drew in a deep breath and started again.

"You were telling me about Lord Chamberlain's brother," I prompted.

Mindy scooped another piece of pizza. I'd already eaten two slices and knew I would be overfull if I ate any more. In contrast, my niece was like a bottomless pit. Jane was keeping pace though, the pair of them eating like it was a competition.

Until DI Munroe brought Jane into the conversation, that is.

"That's how Jane and I met and this is the part that cannot be repeated."

Cued in, Jane dabbed at her lips with a napkin. "Nugent Chamberlain was found on the palace grounds burnt to a crisp inside a device made to fly and shoot fire like a dragon."

"Did you say dragon?" mumbled Mindy, her words almost unintelligible around the pizza in her mouth.

Jane nodded, "A suit made to appear as though a dragon was attacking the palace. It was, of course, a man in a suit."

"The elder of the Duke of Westborough's sons," I said.

DI Munroe jumped in with, "That's just the thing. We found him in the suit, but he couldn't have been flying it." She could see my confusion and continued to explain, "The whole thing was hushed up as you might imagine. Dragons at the palace and members of the royal family burning to death is not the sort of thing that anyone wants to appear on the ten o'clock news. However, in the aftermath it was easy to prove the device did not possess the power to fly with the added weight of a human inside it."

Jane added, "It was riddled with bullet holes too. The soldiers shot at it, but Nugent's body had no bullet holes. He was placed in the device after it crashed. The accelerant employed to produce the fire was a hybrid chemical not too dissimilar to napalm. When it ignited, he burned to death, but he was unconscious before the fire took hold. The autopsy revealed a near-lethal dose of heroin in his bloodstream."

"And you suspect his younger brother?" I was still shaky about why that would be the case.

The women looked inward at each other again.

"We do," DI Munroe replied after a while, "but we don't have any hard evidence."

In a rush of electrical impulses, my brain delivered the reason why they were sitting on my couch: they wanted me to help them get the information they needed. Why me though? In fact, the more I thought about it, the less sense that made. Even with an excuse to visit the palace, I would have no reason to speak to Lord Chamberlain. Anyway, how did they even know I met him today?

Coming down from that cloud of conjecture, I noticed that neither DI Munroe nor Jane were looking my way. They were both looking at Mindy.

Mindy was eyeing the last slice of pizza. When she looked up to see if anyone would challenge her for it, she found three sets of eyes aimed her way.

Recoiling slightly, she said, "Whaaaat?"

It wasn't me they wanted, it was Mindy! Lord Chamberlain made a pass at her and made sure she left with his number.

DI Munroe said, "We need someone who can get close to him. If I ever hope to prove he was behind his brother's death, I need to obtain something ... some piece of evidence that will allow me to justify searching his rooms or seizing his belongings. I ... I'm in a precarious situation at work and one false move will likely end my career."

She chose not to expand on her statement, and I saw no reason to pursue it. I was too focused on what they might be asking my niece to do. Sleep with the handsome royal and search his room while he was asleep? I hardly think so!

"No, I don't think it will need to go *that* far," the detective inspector replied to my unvoiced concerns in a calm voice.

I glanced at my niece, wondering if she was about to say she didn't mind if she had to sleep with him. Not that it's really my business, but I assume she is not a virgin at nineteen. She's had dates with boys and I hear her talking about boys with Philippe, my other assistant, but I cannot recall her ever saying the same boy's name for more than a week at a time. She left me with the impression the men she dated were all a bit rubbish – immature and focused on nothing that interested her.

Anyway, she stayed quiet while DI Munroe explained there was a safe in Lord Chamberlain's living room.

"We're not asking you to do anything that might place you in danger, Mindy. At this time I have nothing to go on other than a long-standing animosity between the brothers and circumstantial evidence – Eddie was the only resident in the palace that night and claimed his brother turned up unannounced. Nugent told me his brother asked him to visit. There are too many things that do not ring true and when the 'dragon' first attacked, killing one of the soldiers a few days before Nugent met his end, Nugent was attending an official event with his father in Leeds. He couldn't have been behind it."

Mindy decided she was having the last piece of pizza anyway. Aiming it at her mouth she paused before biting to ask, "So what do you need me to do? Crack the safe?"

It was Jane who replied.

"DI Munroe is bound by her role and cannot act as she believes she ought without risking termination. If she gets sacked, we lose all hope of catching the killer. I am not held by same restrictions, but I can only gain access to the palace through DI Munroe. So if I get caught she is still for the chop."

"What if Mindy gets caught?" I wanted to know.

"I will be in charge of the investigation," DI Munroe replied. "I'll not lie and say it will not be without complications, but Mindy will not be charged."

"You're sure he's guilty?" Mindy pressed for a definitive answer.

DI Munroe hung her head a little. "Sure? No. That's why we need your help."

"I need you to place this in his room." Jane produced a small plastic bag from her pocket. "It's a simple digital listening device. We will be able to hear everything he says."

Mindy wiped her mouth with a napkin. "You want me to put it in his living room?"

Jane said, "We have been waiting months for an opportunity like this to arise. No one is going to make you do anything, but you could help to catch a killer."

"If he's guilty," said Mindy, reaffirming a point, but resisting her need to say, *'Which I don't think he is.'*

Further conversation was interrupted by the sound of someone kicking my door.

"Felicity! Felicity Philips! I know you're in there! Answer this door so I can kill you!"

Amber

Amber slipped in through the open door because it smelled of a man. Was this where the prince slept? Had she finally found his rooms?

Padding across the carpet she meowed loudly to see if he would hear her and come running. No answer came and she looked about, listening to hear if there was someone around or not.

Her ears caught the faint sound of water running and aiming for it, she went to investigate. Passing by discarded clothing, her nose confirmed she was in the domicile of a man. Whether it was the right man her olfactory system could not discern, but believing she was finally where she wanted to be, she nudged her way through an almost closed door to find herself in a bathroom.

Steam filled it, the human living here taking a shower. Amber was familiar with the process though she did not approve. Using water to wash, be it warm or otherwise, was just unnatural. One's own tongue provided all the cleaning power a creature ever needed; not that Buster ever used his for such a mundane and routine purpose.

Oh, no, the slobbering mutt simply drooled onto the floor and would occasionally use his tongue to lick things: human visitors, the floor if something spilled, snails in the garden, Amber if he could get close enough without her noticing.

She shuddered at a hundred memories and told herself to be glad she'd seen the back of him.

"*No more idiot bulldog for me,*" she chuckled happily.

Backing out of the shower, she returned to the main living space where her nose detected a twang of dog. Nostrils wrinkling, she was horrified to think that her prince might also like dogs. It was bad enough they existed in the first place; though she conceded it was good to have a lesser life form to look down upon, but why would humans ever want to cohabit with them?

"*Hello?*" she meowed again. "*Is there a dog here?*"

No answer came, and semi-satisfied, she crossed the open living space once more, this time heading for the bed. Leaping onto it, she landed amidst a pile of paper and photographs.

Had she been able to read or had the slightest interest in human activities other than those which focused on her and her needs, Amber might have seen the A4 sheet covered in headshots.

The royal family were laid out in neat rows with numbers next to their faces. One was crossed out with bright red pen. It was number forty-six.

The significance would have been lost on Amber even if she had not settled into preening herself in anticipation of the prince returning from the shower. However, the picture of Nugent Chamberlain, eldest son of the Duke of Westborough had particular meaning for the man who slept in the bed on which Amber now washed her face.

The sound of the shower shutting off made Amber stop what she was doing. Turning to face the bathroom door, she batted her eyes and thought about how to present herself: with her tail tucked neatly around her front paws so she looked like a lady, or rolling on her back, coquettishly smiling up at the prince when he walked in.

Unable to decide, she ran out of time, but just as she saw fingers gripping the edge of the door to pull it open from the inside, a spear of horror shot through her heart – something had just moved under the bedcovers and it wasn't a human.

Now caught between her desire to look irresistible for the prince and her mounting worry about what was now fighting to get out from under the thick duvet, she was shocked to her core when a different man came out of the bathroom.

"*Who the heck are you?*" she blurted, backing away from the naked man and unable to keep from glancing at the moving lump under the bedcovers.

Lord Chamberlain hadn't noticed the cat until it squawked which sent a spasm of terror to almost make his feet leave the floor.

Recovering quickly, he swore at the cat. "Go on! Get out!" He flapped an arm at her. Then thought better and rushed to the bed. Tearing off the covers to reveal a miniature dachshund, he said, "Get her, Henkel!"

Ordinarily, Amber would have stood her ground against such a pathetic excuse for a dog. This was not, however, her ground.

Hissing and spitting, she leapt from the bed with the tiny dog in hot pursuit. There was no danger the sausage could catch her, but she nevertheless ran like the devil himself was on her tail.

Watching the cat zip through the gap in his door Lord Chamberlain tutted and called for Henkel to stop.

The miniature dachshund skidded obediently to a halt though he continued to bark until his human passed him to shut and lock the door. Trotting behind Lord Chamberlain's feet as he made his way back to the bedroom for clothes, Henkel heard his human muttering to himself.

"You've got to be more careful, Eddie. Anyone could have walked in." Staring down at the collection of photographs, notes, questions, and diary dates on his bed, Lord Chamberlain shook his head. Killing his older brother while making it look like Nugent was behind his own demise had been easy. Okay, so that odd-looking blonde chick from the Blue Moon Investigation agency almost caught him and he still wasn't convinced she didn't need dealing with, but otherwise the plan went flawlessly.

It moved him one place closer to the throne, but there was a lot of work to do if he was going to make his father the king. Not that he gave two stuffs about dear old daddy. He simply thought it would look better if his father ascended to the throne and he got to succeed him. It wasn't as though the old codger would last much longer.

Settling onto the edge of his bed, he picked up the piece of A4 on which he had laid out the forty-six members of the royal family between him and the throne. One was gone: his older brother. Number forty-five was his father. That left forty-four he needed to take care of.

Quite a few of them were kids, but their deaths wouldn't play on his conscience any more than his brother's. It was necessary. The royal family had been watered down so much over the centuries. His family were true Brits who could trace their line all the way back to King Edward in the late 13th Century, the monarch after whom he was named.

Making a gun with his forefinger and thumb, he aimed it at number seventeen and mimed shooting Princess Anne's son, Philip.

"I think you should be next. No one will miss you, Phil."

Tidying the papers into a bundle, Lord Eddie Chamberlain locked them securely inside his safe and whistling a happy tune, started to get dressed for dinner.

ULTIMATUMS

"**F**elishity! Answer the door!"

Buster had gone from snoring to barking in less than a second. There was someone being loud outside my door, and he wanted to kill them.

That the voice screaming obscenities through my letterbox belonged to Primrose Green was in no doubt whatsoever. Mindy recognised it too. However, DI Munroe heard the threat to my life and reacted as one might expect a police officer would – she was on her way to the door and moving with purpose.

"You know who that is?" she asked as she left the room.

I had to run to stop her getting to Primrose first. Hooking DI Munroe's elbow and getting between her and the door, I said, "It's my arch-rival, Primrose Green. She lost the wedding contract this morning as you know. She is clearly a little upset. I just need to talk to her. She's not going to do anything to hurt me."

"Felishity! You vile cow! I'm gonna cut your throat!"

DI Munroe raised an eyebrow. "I can arrest her just for saying that and she sounds drunk."

Once Mindy had Buster under control, I reached behind my back for the doorknob. With a twist, the door opened and I turned to face my rival.

"Aarrrrrgggh!" she screamed, raising a tyre iron above her head as she charged at me.

I squealed in fright, but Primrose stopped before the police officer could get around me to tackle her.

The rage in Primrose's face melted away and she started to sob.

"Why, Felicity? Why stoop so low? My husband walked out!" she snarled, her emotions changing gear every few seconds. "He had no idea the pictures existed, and I was never going to tell him."

I wanted to go to her, but she still had the tyre iron in her right hand.

DI Munroe pushed me gently to one side and stepped out of the house. Holding up her warrant card, she said, "Drop the weapon now, please, Mrs Green."

Noticing the police officer for the first time, Primrose recognised her. "What are you doing here? Oh, my God, are you all in it together?"

"The weapon, Mrs Green. I will not warn you again."

Primrose followed DI Munroe's gaze and looked surprised to find the iron bar in her hand. It clattered to the ground a moment later and she started to sob again. "I won, Felicity. I won fair and square. Why did you have to take it from me?"

"I didn't," I replied, hoping the tone of my voice would help to convey the truth. "I had nothing to do with it."

"Liar!" Primrose screeched.

To my left, Mindy was standing relaxed yet poised, her silent vigil leaving her ready to deal with Primrose should she choose to attack after all.

I didn't think she was going to though, and more than anything else, I felt sorry for her. Had her husband really walked out? I guess it wouldn't be a shock if that were the case.

Holding out a hand, I wiggled my fingers – a sign that she should come with me.

"Let's talk about it inside, Primrose. Maybe together we can figure out who did this to you."

Her head, bowed as she cried, snapped back up to glare at me.

"You did it!" she screamed again.

"Mrs Green I must ask you to lower your voice," insisted DI Munroe.

Primrose either didn't hear or just didn't care.

"You did it, Felicity! You just couldn't stand being second. Well I'm going to get you for what you did ..."

DI Munroe stepped into Primrose's personal space, their faces inches apart.

"Have you been drinking, Mrs Green?"

The question refocused Primrose, an alarm sounding somewhere in her brain.

"No," she lied.

"Yes, you have, Mrs Green," Munroe was in full cop mode now. "And is that your car?"

Left at a bad angle, half on the pavement outside my house, Primrose's car looked abandoned rather than parked.

Primrose swivelled around to look at it and almost fell when the rotation caused her to stumble.

"Okay, that's enough," DI Munroe reached for Primrose, steadying her before she fell. At least, I thought that was what she was doing. I was wrong though. Munroe had switched back into detective inspector mode and was performing an arrest.

Now I have no love for Primrose Green, goodness knows I have every reason to loathe her, but I wasn't the engineer of her downfall and the empathy I felt made me fight for her.

"... right to remain silent. Anything you do say ..."

"Stop!" My raised voice got Munroe's attention. The detective inspector had her phone in her left hand. With her right she gripped Primrose's arm, and she was going to call for someone to take her away if I didn't intervene. "Stop." I repeated more calmly. "There's nothing to gain by arresting her."

"She drove here under the influence of alcohol, behaved in a threatening manner, and that's just for starters."

"We won't help you if you arrest her." I'm not the kind of person who delivers ultimatums. I'm not sure I have ever done so before in my life. Moreover, I couldn't find the words to explain what was going through my head right now, but I didn't want to see Primrose taken away in a police car and if I had to use leverage to achieve that, I would.

DI Munroe fixed me with a look that warned me not to say another word.

Punctuating the moment in her own, unique way, Primrose chose that moment to throw up on my driveway.

Speaking to Munroe, I held my nerve and reinforced how I felt. "I mean it. Let her go."

Mindy came up behind me. "Auntie, what are you doing?" Her voice was incredulous though whether she was more shocked by my decision to challenge the police officer or my desire to help a sworn enemy I could not tell.

Munroe stepped away, releasing Primrose's arm – it wasn't like she was going to run off.

Feet moving fast as she rushed toward me, her face like thunder, she got close enough to whisper though her voice came out as a growl.

"Mrs Philips, might I remind you that I am a senior police officer. Strong-arming me would be ill-advised to say the least."

With my own voice barely above a whisper, I said, "You want my niece to spy on a member of the royal family and take part in what I suspect to be an illegal operation. I want Primrose Green to go free. Quid pro quo I believe." How I wasn't stuttering defied explanation, but then another thought popped into my head. "Also, you're not to do anything about the missing sapphire."

Munroe made a scoffing noise, unable to believe what I was asking.

"Those are my terms. You only know about the sapphire by accident. You need to give me enough time to figure out what happened before you act."

DI Munroe squinted at me. She's a short woman, shorter than me, and I don't meet all that many people who have to look up at me.

"Very well, Mrs Philips. I'll give you two days to find the sapphire. After that, I will be speaking to Mr Smallbridge." She came a step closer, getting right inside my personal space. "And rest assured, I will not forget this incident." As veiled threats go it was a good one, for I had no idea what her statement meant, only that it was trouble.

With a final look of disgust aimed at Primrose, who now had a hand against the wall of my house to keep herself upright, DI Munroe confirmed Mindy had the device from Jane and knew what was expected of her.

Brushing the incident with Primrose aside, she said, "There should be nothing difficult about this task. All Mindy needs to do is convince Lord Chamberlain to invite her inside his rooms. The device can be placed almost anywhere and it will pick up his voice. Once that is done, she can make her excuse and leave again."

I checked with Mindy. "Are you sure about this?"

She shrugged like it was nothing. "Sure. I still don't think he's guilty of doing anything wrong, let alone murdering his brother. But I'll plant your device if it helps to get you off his back."

Her stance on the subject was much like a slap to the face for the investigative work the two detectives had carried out, but they let it go without comment.

"You're going back tomorrow?" DI Munroe asked though it sounded more like an instruction.

This seemed like a good time to bring up my Amber situation.

"Your cat is loose in the palace?" Munroe repeated what I said with disbelief. "Okay, I'll find out if anyone has seen her. I guess that could help to give us reason for you to be poking about. I'll expect to see you early tomorrow."

Jane bade us a goodnight and left with DI Munroe, the two women taking separate cars. I looked up at the sound of a muscular engine starting and was a tad surprised to see the willowy blonde with the Adam's apple driving away in a powerful-looking Aston Martin.

As quiet settled, I felt a frown forming on my brow – I still had Primrose to deal with.

HOUSe GUeST

Primrose didn't want to come into my house, didn't want my hospitality or kindness and certainly not my sympathy, but she had too little resistance left to fight as Mindy and I guided her inside.

While Mindy took Primrose's keys and did a better job of parking her car, I settled Primrose onto my couch and went to make strong coffee. I returned a few minutes later to discover my unexpected 'guest' was asleep. She'd kicked off her shoes and was snoring lightly, her mouth open and her head lolling to one side.

She was an attractive woman who presented herself as close to physically flawless every time I saw her.

Except now.

An evil voice at the back of my head suggested I take some photographs and video footage of her. Releasing that on top of the awful pictures already circulating would finish her off and, reputation in ruins, she would cease to be a thorn in my side.

However, while I knew it was a tactic Primrose might employ were the tables to be turned, I could not stoop so low. I had rescued her from the police, quite why I was yet to fathom, but now that she was in my care I needed to do all I could to restore her.

Fetching a blanket, I covered her and hoped she would sleep off whatever she had foolishly imbibed. Closing the door behind me, I found Mindy with Buster in the kitchen.

Leaning against the kitchen door for support when I closed that too, I closed my eyes and muttered, "I need a gin."

Mindy laughed, "Staying at your house is fun, Auntie. It's rarely dull."

Buster wagged his tail. "*How about something from the box of biscuits?*"

I acquiesced to Buster's request, throwing him an extra large Bonio which he caught and crunched before it could hit the floor. I heard him devour it as I crossed to the fridge to find tonic water and ice.

I was almost there when the doorbell rang.

Mindy frowned. "You think they forgot something?"

That it was DI Munroe returning was my first thought too, but I was wrong.

It was Edward Smallbridge.

And he was holding a big bunch of flowers.

"Good evening, Felicity, dear. I'm sorry to show up unannounced like this. I won't come in if it's inconvenient."

Inconvenient? I was starting to feel like I couldn't tell which way was up.

Backing away from the door, I invited him in. "We're in the kitchen," I let him know. He didn't need to know why. "Can I offer you a drink?"

"Oh, just some water, thank you. I don't like to drink and drive."

"I got these for you, Felicity, as a thank you for coming to my rescue." He handed over the flowers, a hand tied bouquet of lilies and irises, not something he'd picked up at a supermarket. "I was in such a panic when I called you that I failed to consider what else you might need to be doing with your time. These are to say thank you for dropping whatever it was to help an old fool."

Mindy slid off her stool at the breakfast bar, "I'll, um, leave you to it," she said, dipping her head at Edward on her way out and hooking Buster's collar to drag him along.

Edward gave her a smile, but seemed pleased that she was leaving.

I wasn't so sure I wanted her to go, but couldn't see a way to make her stay without it looking odd. Edward was an old friend, however his recent expression of romantic interest had me on edge now that we were alone together.

Was it okay for me to be interested? I still couldn't figure out how to enter a new relationship. I had been on dates with Vince, but it wouldn't be accurate to say we were dating; such a term comes with other connotations.

Edward was handsome, the right age, had money, didn't have kids, had never been married. Had Vince not interrupted our dinner the one time we sat down to talk, where might Edward and I now be? Ok, so I still believed he was going to propose that night – he took out a ring box right before Vince did his thing to halt proceedings – but maybe that was never his intention. That would be ridiculous, right?

I should probably ask and get it out into the open, but I'm just not that brave.

Edward reached up to fetch a vase down from the top of my kitchen cupboards – I usually have to get a stool – and we talked while I arranged the flowers.

"Thank you, Edward, these are lovely. You really didn't have to."

"Of course I did, Felicity. It's the least I can do. I must ask, and I'm sorry to push, will you be able to go back to the palace tomorrow? I know you've said detective work isn't your forte, but you cannot deny the results you have been able to achieve."

Yes, because of my cat and dog.

When I said nothing, he asked, "Were you able to get a hold of Mr Slater?"

Drat. I still hadn't contacted him.

"No, Edward. With one thing and another, I am yet to call him. However, I feel confident I can get him to come to the palace tomorrow." My response was enough to placate him.

"Oh, good. Good. Super." Edward both looked and sounded distracted, like there were questions in his head he could not work out how to pose. I didn't want to nudge him to reveal what he was thinking and didn't have to for he found is voice. "The two of you are still dating?"

"Yes," I replied, my automatic response startling me. *Had I meant to say that?*

"Good," he smiled though the joy he expressed failed to reach his eyes. I guess he was disappointed, and I wrestled with what I ought to say. "Good. Super. I'm so pleased for you both."

"It's not serious," I managed to say, but the words lacked conviction and if anything were confusing given my previous response. "What I mean to say is, we are going on dates, but I wouldn't say we were dating."

Edward cocked an eyebrow. "That sounds like splitting hairs to me, Felicity. What are you trying to say?"

Good question.

Now that I had dug a hole and was standing firmly in it, was it best to say nothing at all? Or should I attempt to explain how I found myself holding Vince at bay because I wasn't sure I wanted to be in a relationship with anyone?

Remembering something I'd heard on TV, I ventured, "It's complicated?"

"But you are sleeping with him?" Edward asked, making my mouth drop open.

"Edward!"

He held up both hands in supplication. "I'm sorry, Felicity. I have no idea where that came from. Please forgive me. Your sex life is none of my business." Patting his pockets to make sure he had all his belongings, Edward backed toward the kitchen door. "I, ah ... I ought to be going. Apologies again for the intrusion."

I wanted to clearly state I was not sleeping with Vince, nor had I allowed anyone into my bed (unless one counts Amber's regular night time intrusions) since Archie passed. I didn't though. Keeping quiet and letting Edward leave was by far the best thing I could do.

Was I sleeping with Vince? What a thing to ask.

At the door, Edward paused to let me catch up and apologised again for his unannounced arrival and his rudeness.

"Edward, I think it best if we just put it behind us and never speak of it again."

Edward nodded in agreement. Standing outside on my doormat where a slight drizzle was just starting, he asked, "You are still willing to help an old fool in his hour of need?"

With a sigh I exhaled through my nose, I said, "Yes, Edward. I will call Vince shortly and between us I am sure we will be able to either eliminate Lord Chamberlain as the thief, or prove it was him." Vince was resourceful and capable; if the handsome royal took the sapphire, Vince would find the evidence.

"I'm afraid I won't be at the palace at all tomorrow; the King's coronation is taking up a lot of my time as you might imagine and I will be in my shop all day." Edward thrust out his hand for me to shake and left me to mull over the confusing thoughts in my head.

MODERN DATING RULES

After Edward left, I spent twenty minutes holding my phone and specifically not calling Vince. It was late on a Saturday and I had no idea what he might be doing. Would he be on a date with another woman? Surely not, but I had to admit I'd not given him much reason to hang around waiting for me. More importantly, how would I feel if he was? Hurt? Betrayed? Indifferent?

I couldn't work it out. Of course, assuming he was at home, which he might very well be, what was I going to say to him? It was close to bedtime, but arguably that was still hours away if one was a night owl. Would he think I was calling to invite him over even though I would explain my need to take him to the palace? Would he insist on coming to my house anyway because he wanted to discuss my proposal face to face?

What would that be like? Our dates so far had been on neutral ground at a bar or restaurant. Knowing what kind of rogue Vince Slater was, I could easily envisage him accidentally spilling a drink down his shirt and needing to take it off, then 'accidentally' having just a touch too much wine and saying he couldn't possibly drive home.

Ha! Well, I had Primrose on my couch, I remembered, so he couldn't come over.

No, that didn't work because he would then suggest we chat in the kitchen which was where we had always congregated in the past whenever he had chosen to visit uninvited. Plus, Vince would suggest he should just sleep in my bed next to me. He would promise to behave and of course he would and despite knowing that I wouldn't get a wink of sleep all night.

Eventually, when my brain began to ache from all the permutations it was trying to compute, I sent him a text message.

'*Vince, can you come to Buckingham Palace with me tomorrow? I have been given the royal wedding contract and have need of a person with detective skills. Can explain on the way. They want me there after breakfast in the morning.*'

It took me five minutes to get the message to read the way I wanted, and I still hesitated before pressing the send button.

When my phone pinged ten seconds later, I almost dropped it.

'*Can't do first thing. I have a prior engagement. How about after lunch?*'

I squinted at the phone. What could have Vince so tied up he wouldn't drop it to help me? I wanted to enquire, but knew that would be little different from Edward asking about my sex life.

Was he with another woman and would need a lie in? Was that it? I had no good reason to care and yet I did.

When I took so long replying that Vince sent a follow-up text to confirm I got the first one, I finally bit the bullet.

'Yes, that's fine, thank you. Please come to mine when you are free. We can travel in one car.'

I slept fitfully, dreams of Vince in bed with other women haunting my sleep to make fun of my emotional insecurity. Waking with a grumpy face and frown that would yield extra wrinkles if I wasn't careful, I was a little shocked to see the time shown on my bedside clock – it was way past my usual time to be up.

This was entirely to do with not having Amber around to climb on my chest and pat my face because she wanted her breakfast.

I've tried shutting the bedroom door, but that just results in her meowing loudly outside until I give in and feed her.

A pang of sorrow shot through my heart at her absence though I told myself I would be getting her back today. She wasn't going to be allowed to stay at the palace no matter what her thoughts on the matter might be, and once I got her home, I felt certain she would be happy to be here.

Fairly certain.

Well, she was coming home to live with me whether she liked it or not.

With a gasp, I remembered Primrose was sleeping on my couch and rushed to wrap a robe around myself.

There was no one in the lounge and the blanket I'd placed over her sleeping form was neatly folded and placed on the arm of the couch.

Mindy's voice drifted through the house, "She left more than an hour ago. She wasn't happy."

Wasn't happy? With me? I told her I had nothing to do with the leaked pictures, but I guess it shouldn't come as a shock that she didn't believe me.

I found Mindy in the kitchen eating breakfast. She wore her usual combination of stretchy black sports clothing, and had clearly been exercising.

"Did you speak to her before she left?"

Mindy's fork paused halfway to her mouth. "Not exactly. She came out of the bathroom just as I was getting up, so she couldn't exactly avoid me. I said good morning, and she told me to 'go to hell'. I think she is holding a grudge about the photographs."

"But I didn't leak them to the press!"

"If you say so, Auntie. I can see where she might get the idea you did though. You're the one who immediately benefitted from her losing the royal wedding contract."

Coffee was needed. Muttering about taking the blame for crimes I hadn't committed, I asked, "Did she say anything else?"

"Not really. Said something about this not being over and how she was going to prove you leaked the pictures and drag you through the courts for it." Mindy finished her sentence and stuffed another forkful of food into her mouth – she was like an eating machine.

What was I supposed to do about Primrose? I wanted to call her and attempt to have a conversation, yet I could recognise her wounds were too deep, too raw, and too fresh for her to see reason. She could look for the evidence to prove I was behind her downfall, but I wasn't, so she would come up empty. I still wondered if Edward was behind it, engineering things to place me in a position where I could help with his missing jewel.

I had no idea how to broach that subject either. Running through things in my head, I noticed the pile of food on Mindy's plate. Demonstrating her cast iron, teenager's ability to absorb calories, her plate sported no less than four pieces of toast plus sausage, bacon, beans, and eggs.

"Where do you put all that?"

She cleared her mouth with a swig of tea and said, "In my belly!" like it was a thing to be proud of. "I'm hungry and I don't want my belly to be rumbling later when I am out with Eddie."

I was lifting the kettle across to fill it at the sink and almost dropped it when I spun around to see if she was serious.

Seeing my expression, she had to fight to swallow what was in her mouth so she could say, "What? Isn't there this whole plan for me to date him so I can plant a bug in his room?"

"You didn't call him, did you?"

"No," she frowned like I was being ridiculous. "I sent him a text."

It was like reeling from punches. I know girls are much more forward now than they used to be in my day and many of my friends in the eighties were willing to be the one to chase the boy they liked, but that sort of behaviour still came with certain labels even then.

"Auntie you look like you sat on a hedgehog." Her fork came halfway to her mouth before she dropped it and jumped off her chair, a look of panic in her eyes. "Oh, my God! Auntie, you're having a stroke. I need to get you to lie down. Dammit, what's the acronym for treating a stroke victim?"

I slapped her hands away as she came near.

"I am not having a stroke! I just ... you caught me by surprise is all." Placing the kettle on the kitchen counter, I tried to keep the incredulity from my voice when I said, "You sent a member of the royal family a text message to ask him out on a date?"

Mindy wandered back to her seat and forked a piece of sausage into her mouth. "Sure," she replied with a shrug. "Why wouldn't I? He might have been born with a silver spoon up his bum ..."

"In his mouth."

"Huh?"

"In his mouth. The saying is that a posh person has been born with a silver spoon in his mouth, not up his bum." I could feel the muscle by my right eye twitching again.

Mindy shrugged. "Whatever. My point is he's just a guy at the end of the day, royalty or not, and since he gave me his number, it falls to me to make the first move, that's how it works. Or rather, he already made the first move in giving me his number. Messaging him or not is then down to me, but the invitation to do so is implied."

I guess that made sense.

"I'm having lunch with him." I would have spat out my false teeth if I had any. I couldn't make up my mind about the two men who were clearly interested in me and generally thought it would be simpler to just spend the rest of my life alone, yet my niece was messaging members of the royal family to arrange lunch dates. "Some place called Claridge's. Have you heard of it?"

A tired laugh escaped my lips. "Yes, Mindy, it's only one of the most exclusive places in London."

"Oh, I'll wear knickers then."

I had no idea what to make of that statement, but a thought occurred to me. "You need to plant the bug in his room. How are you going to do that if you are having lunch at Claridge's?"

She shrugged again, her focus not on me but on her phone. "I doubt it will be difficult to get him to take me back to his place, Auntie."

It's a good thing I'm not her mother. Like a gong sounding in my head, I realised what was missing.

"Where's your mum?"

"Didn't come home last night."

Well, either Shane murdered her or they figured some things out and were back together. I hoped for the latter.

Mindy intended to spend the morning getting ready – I guess it's not everyday one gets to have lunch with a member of the royal family in a high end London club. That took care of her, so walking Buster around the village and letting him run with the other dogs at the park, I thought about what I wanted to do with my morning.

The one thing I couldn't shift was my desire to know what Vince was up to. Maybe it was caused by spending too much time with my youthful and reckless niece, but I was giving serious consideration to inviting the dangerous rogue on a date. There was something about being the one to organise it that appealed.

Perhaps it was no more complicated than knowing I would be setting the terms. I was attracted to him. I liked the way he smiled and the scent of his cologne. There were many, many positive attributes, but the same could be said about Edward.

If I wasn't to spend the rest of my life alone, I needed to 'put myself out there' a term Mindy once employed. First, I wanted to know if Vince was doing something work related this morning, or whether he was, indeed, with another woman.

I might tell the world I am not a sleuth, but I could manage to snoop on Vince Slater.

I had already called DI Munroe to let her know I would not be at the palace until after lunch, and that Mindy had successfully arranged to meet Lord Chamberlain – I couldn't quite get myself to refer him as Eddie even in my own head.

Amber was still at large inside the palace and had been spotted, but not caught, by numerous members of the staff. At least I knew she was there and probably safe.

With all those boxes ticked, I led Buster home – I was going to visit Vince's house and see what there was to see.

SPYING

Vince lives in a nice, detached house in East Farleigh, not too far from me. I know this because I dropped him off once after he'd come to my rescue for the umpteenth time.

I drove there in my Mercedes with the roof up in deference to the cold air outside. Buster rode shotgun in the passenger seat, the belt looped through his collar and around his body. I had to constantly remind him to close his mouth so he didn't drool too much on the seat, but he insisted on sitting up straight so he could see out of the window.

This meant he could see cows and sheep and other interesting things which he wanted to bark at. That, apparently, included a cyclist.

I should have known it was about to happen because Buster said, "*Watch this*," in the instant before launching himself at the window barking like a rabid idiot when I cruised past the cyclist on a country lane.

The poor cyclist, a man in his forties wearing all the gear, jerked in shock, lost control, and crashed into the soft verge at the side of the road.

Buster sniggered, laughing at his practical joke until I told him off.

"That was dangerous, Buster." He hung his head and looked ashamed as only a dog can. Stopping the car, I checked the rear-view and re-versed back.

The man was on his feet by then, and looked not to be injured though he was picking bits of hedgerow out of his helmet.

I was talking as I got out of the car. "I'm so terribly sorry." It felt like I was doing a lot of apologising recently. "He's not normally like that."

The man waved me to silence. "It's not like I can hold you to account. I have dogs myself. I don't recall them ever scaring a person off their bike before, but they're no angels."

Making sure the man was okay and offering to pay for any damage to his bike – which he refused – ate up a few minutes, but I wasn't on a schedule so it hardly mattered. Pulling away, I checked he was moving again before putting him from my mind and returning to my thoughts about Vince, the palace, Lord Chamberlain, Edward, and his missing sapphire.

The thing is, I should have been thinking about the royal wedding and nothing else. It was a mammoth undertaking for which I could justify taking on additional staff. They would be temporary hires, but I was being paid what Primrose bid for the job which was a fat percentage higher than the budget I proposed. It told me I had something to learn from my rival.

Arriving at Vince's house, I parked across the street behind a battered old Austin Allegro. It was an awful brown colour where rust hadn't eaten the bodywork away and it listed to one side.

Right, what now, Felicity?

Buster looked at me expectantly. "*Are we getting out?*"

I scrunched my face in thought. Coming to spy on Vince sounded like a good idea when I was at home imagining him canoodling with some younger woman, but parked across the street, I felt like an idiot.

Thinking the only sensible thing to do was leave, I almost wet myself when someone knocked on the window right next to my head.

Buster barked, "*Oh, hey, it's Vince! Hello Vince!*" He was on his feet on the passenger seat, pulling against the seatbelt with his tail wagging so hard it whacked against the dashboard.

Buster was right in that it was Vince, and I had been right to guess that he was with another woman.

Powering down my window, I squinted up at the eighty-something-year-old lady on his arm.

"Hello," I offered, sounding more than a little unconvincing because my brain defied my demand to supply a plausible reason for being parked facing his house on a Sunday morning.

"Good morning, Felicity." Vince turned to speak to the old lady. "Mother, this is Felicity?"

Oh, dear Lord, he's out with his mother and if I had to guess I would say he was on his way to church.

Vince's mother's brow crinkled for a moment, but her eyes brightened, and a smile came to her face when she said, "Oh, this is the one you're always talking about. Oh, it's so lovely to finally meet her. You rogue, Vince. You didn't say she was joining us for church this morning."

Vince was always talking about me? To his mother?

Reeling from that one, I was staring dumbfounded at her for so long she nudged her son and asked, "Is she all right?"

Snapping back to the here and now, I apologised - it sure was apology season – and got out of the car.

"*Hey what about me?*" barked Buster, causing me to duck back inside to set him free. The dopey bulldog bounced across my seat and onto the pavement where his tail wagged so hard he could hardly stand. "*Hi, Vince! Hi! Who's this? Does anyone have any snacks for me?*"

"Hello. It's so lovely to meet you," I shook Vince's mum's hand.

"And you, dear. Vince has such lovely things to say about you. I do hope you'll make an honest man of him. Goodness knows I've waited long enough."

I felt colour rising in my cheeks.

Equally embarrassed, Vince said, "Mother we have talked about this. You can't just marry me off to the first woman who looks my way."

"Well someone should, Vince. Goodness knows I've missed out on grandchildren. Now," she turned her attention on me. "You must call me Ethel. And who is this lovely young fellow?"

Buster's tail, already wagging so fast a human eye couldn't see it, doubled in speed now that attention had swung his way.

"*I'm Buster!*" barked Buster, his exuberance making him bounce his front paws off the ground. "*I know I look like an ordinary bulldog, but I have an alter ego through whom I fight crime. Obviously, I can't tell you my secret superhero name, but chances are you've heard of me.*"

"This is Buster," I explained since I was certain I was the only one hearing his voice. I chose to ignore the part about Devil Dog.

"We'll have to get moving, Vince," his mother said. "I don't like to be late. You are coming with us, aren't you, dear?"

I said, "Um," and looked at Vince. "I didn't really think this through," I lied, pretending I was there to attend church. "I don't think I can take Buster in with me."

"Oh, you can leave him at Vince's house. He can run around the garden. That's okay, isn't it, Vince?" said Ethel, framing it like a question even though it sounded like an order.

Vince met my eyes with a very deliberate smile. A smile that made it quite clear he knew I was outside his house to spy on him and would be paying an as yet unspecified forfeit for my deception.

"Of course," Vince replied, his shark-infested smile rigidly applied. "Whyever would I not want an energetic dog running riot around my house and garden?"

Buster was pleased enough with the arrangement and since it was on the way, we left Ethel at Vince's gate to stop in and drop him off. Leaving the front door open, Vince led me inside.

It was my first time inside his abode, and I couldn't help but look around as I walked through the front door. Vince lived in a detached cottage which looked to be a three-bedroom place built in the late nineteenth century. The front door was arranged symmetrically between two sash windows with two more set directly above them and a smaller window a few feet above the door where I guessed the stairs met the top floor.

Inside, the house was neat and tidy with lots of old wooden furniture. It looked comfortable and lived in and the whole place smelled of Vince.

Buster shot off the moment I let him off his lead to explore. Essentially, he was doing the same as me but with vastly more energy and excitement.

Vince hustled through the house to the kitchen where I heard him filling a pan with water.

"He'll be okay with a saucepan?" his voice echoed.

"Sure. Thank you."

Startling me, Vince appeared from the other direction; there was a circuit through his house, the dining and living rooms connected at the back by the kitchen or a hallway.

"Oh, don't thank me yet, darling. Let's wait and see how much destruction he causes." He fixed me with a pair of narrowed eyes. "I feel I should check before we get to church ..."

"Yes?" What was he going to ask me?

"Well, you won't burst into flames as you cross the threshold or anything like that, will you?" Seeing my bewilderment, he said, "You know, from all the lies you've told already this morning."

Feeling my face flush, I was about to apologise, when he stepped inside my guard and kissed me full on the mouth. We were still in the open doorway of his house and in full view of his mother.

"You owed me that at the very least," he grinned and winked as he took my hand.

I had just enough time to yell, "Be good, Buster! Don't break anything!" before Vince shut the door and hurried me back down the garden path – we were going to church.

Jealous Eyes

A fter the service we took refreshments with many of the other parishioners in an adjoining hall. Three ladies in their seventies had tea and cake and other things for sale from a small kitchen in the corner.

Ethel nattered with about a dozen other ladies her age or thereabouts, the lot of them gathered in a raggedy circle of chairs around two small tables pushed together. They all had tea or coffee, and most had a slice of cake.

Vince had a bacon sandwich. "I got in late last night," he explained. "One of the lads got hurt on a security op."

"He was attacked?" I knew Vince's firm ran bodyguard details for minor celebrities and persons who felt they needed protection.

Vince chuckled. "No, he tripped and twisted his ankle. He had to go to hospital for an x-ray and the chaps with him had to stay with the principal. It was no big deal, but I got home late and missed dinner."

"Oh, I see."

Finishing his last bite, Vince set his plate on the table to his right and slurped his coffee before saying, "So what were you hoping to see this morning? Another woman leaving my place?"

"No." I was too quick to answer and unconvincing to boot. Also, I was lying in church and that had to be bad. Heat radiating off my cheeks, I admitted the truth. "Yes. Kind of. I don't know, Vince."

He nodded and met my eyes with a sincere look. "It's okay Felicity. You want to trust me, but you're not sure you should. I say all the right things, but you're not going to be carefree with your affections and need reassurances before you get too deeply involved."

How does he do that? It was not the first time he had peeled apart exactly how I was feeling and laid it out as if my emotions were written on my face.

When I failed to find a response, he said, "I hope this morning has helped to alleviate your concerns. I am exactly what I say I am, Felicity. I will give you all my love if you will let me."

There he goes again, saying all the right things. And what man talks like that? Archie never did in three decades of marriage.

Swirling along on his river of confusion – to be fair, the confusion was all mine, he just created it, I was caught off guard when he changed the subject.

"Now, what are we doing at the palace? You said you have the royal wedding contract now. I take it you found the pictures of Primrose and sent them to the press to get her out of the way."

"No!" I recoiled in horror. "Why does everyone think that? I would never do something so callous."

Vince gave me an 'if you say so' shrug.

"I don't know who released the pictures, but with Primrose out of the picture, they called me to step in. That's not what I need you for, obviously. You remember Edward Smallbridge? My jeweller friend I was having dinner with when you decided to pretend to be a waiter?"

Vince acted like he needed to rack his brains to recall the incident and I thought he was going to lie about it until he said, "Oh, yes. Kind of chubby, not very good-looking, was going to propose on your first date and is probably a serial killer. That guy? What about him?"

I rolled my eyes. "Edward is charming, good-looking, doesn't mess with my head, and I don't know that he was going to propose because *someone*," I ground my teeth together, "interrupted him before he could. Anyway, he's the jeweller appointed to the royal family and with the king's coronation just a few weeks away, he's been cleaning and checking some of the jewels." I looked around and lowered my voice. "A priceless sapphire was taken from a tiara while it was in his care, and he thinks a member of the royal family has it. The person was there at the time it vanished. He's in dire straits and wants help to get it back."

"And he called you?" Vince sounded sceptical.

"Yes," I frowned at his unspoken suggestion I was the wrong person for the job. "And specifically asked that I get hold of you. He wants this cleared up quickly and quietly. He can't go to the police and accuse a member of the royal household without solid evidence. He's hoping we can get it."

"And you have access to the palace?"

I nodded. "I'm expected back there today. Oh, and Amber is there so I have a legitimate reason to be wandering the halls looking for her."

Vince's eyebrows rose – he was impressed. "Sounds like you've got most of it worked out. Well, I was planning to watch the rugby this afternoon, but I suppose spending time with you does sound more enticing."

He was teasing me, and I was waiting for him to attach a condition to his assistance. He didn't, but he did lean in so he could kiss me again. The light peck on the lips was seen by anyone who cared to be looking our way. That included Ethel who nudged the woman next to her and said something that made a whole gang of them cackle.

That brought fresh colour to my cheeks, but it was the hard eyes of half a dozen or more women all glaring at me that caught my attention. They saw Vince kiss me and didn't like it. Were they all after him? Surely not. The women were all in their forties or fifties and a variety of shapes and sizes, though none could be considered unattractive. Vince was a wealthy single man in a church congregation and I guess that made him hot property.

Feeling uncomfortable, I murmured, "We should go as soon as we can."

Vince put down his coffee mug. "I'm ready when you are?"

"What about your mother?"

"Oh, she'll be here until they kick her out and always goes to the pub after church with her friends unless she is having dinner with me."

The matter settled, Vince kissed his mother's cheek and promised to speak to her soon; we were off to London.

HUNTED

Amber was becoming distressed by her inability to find the prince. The palace was too big, that was one conclusion she was unhappy to draw. Hungry now, having missed dinner last night and breakfast this morning, she was further distressed at being separated from her litter tray.

So far, she been forced to use two large potted plants to do her business and the whole palace experience was beginning to wear thin.

Her stomach gurgled its emptiness yet again. It sounded loud in the silent hallway.

"*Where is he?*" she complained.

The prince had been so lovely, and he smelled wonderful. Amber thought perhaps she would need to get rid of the woman he had with him; she was completely superfluous to their relationship and likely to just get in the way of their love.

That was all moot if she couldn't find him.

Little did she know Prince Marcus did not live at the palace. Few royals ever do, so she could search forever, but she would not find him.

Not ready to give up, and unsure how she could go back to Felicity if she did, Amber pushed on. Unfortunately, among the list of things she didn't know, was that she was being stalked.

One floor beneath her, two of the Queen's corgis were sniffing the wall.

"*Here's another one,*" said Misfit, his nose dissecting Buster's mark.

Nudging in next to him, Sandy said, "*It's the same as the others.*"

"*That bulldog from the other day,*" snarled Sandy's sister, Candy.

"*What was he thinking?*" Misfit voiced what the others were thinking. "*Marking our territory like he could claim it for himself. If he ever shows his face here again ...*"

Bounding into the corridor, two more corgis came to join their pack-members.

"*You'll never guess what Muriel found on the next floor!*" squeaked Elton.

Sandy, Candy, and Misfit looked up from the scent mark on the wall. No one said anything for several seconds.

Bored of waiting, Candy asked, "*Well?*"

Confused, Elton, blinked, "*Well what?*"

"*You were telling us what Muriel found upstairs, you nitwit,*" said Sandy.

Elton frowned and thought about widdling in Sandy's bed when he wasn't looking; he had too much attitude by half.

"*No,*" Elton explained "*I encouraged you to guess. You haven't guessed.*"

"*Oh, for goodness sake,*" sighed Muriel, pushing her way around Elton. "*There's a cat.*"

"*A cat!*" spat Sandy, Candy, and Misfit all at once.

"*A female cat,*" said Elton, too excited to keep the news any longer. "*So, extra snarky. She's been all over the first floor.*"

Misfit placed his paws deliberately, adopting what he believed to be his purposeful stance.

"*Get the rest of the gang,*" he growled, his voice deep and foreboding. "*This is a cat-free palace. There's never been a cat here on my watch.*"

Candy tilted her head to one side. "*Are you sure it's a cat, Muriel?*"

Muriel cocked an eyebrow. "*You think I don't know cat poop when I taste it? I left some if you want to try for yourself.*" Her remark was sufficient to settle the matter. There was a cat in the palace and they were going to find it. What happened when they did would come down to the cat.

LUNCH DATE

By the time Vincent was driving up the A2 to London with Felicity in the passenger seat and Buster asleep in the back, Mindy was stepping off the train at Oxford Circus Tube Station. A small fluttering of nerves gripped her, and she placed a hand to her core as though that might send the unsettling feeling away.

Meeting a boy for a date was no big deal in her mind, but this wasn't just any boy and they were not going for pizza in Maidstone. Mindy felt like she was about as far outside her comfort zone as she could be.

Eddie was meeting her here, outside the station so she wouldn't have to walk into Claridge's by herself. Mindy would never openly admit the thought of approaching somewhere so posh was daunting, but that was the truth of it.

Lifting her phone to her ear – calling rather than send a text – she heard Eddie's voice before her call could even connect.

"Mindy!"

She looked to her left to find him approaching through the crowd. A head taller than most, the handsome royal was easy to pick from the press of pedestrians all around him and the smile on his face went straight through her like a lightning bolt aimed at her libido.

Tracking his left arm – she could see he was holding something – she spotted a sausage dog on a lead. Dachshunds were literally her favourite dog.

She raised an arm to wave back, only getting halfway before he was coming up to her. He reached out to touch her shoulder and leaned down to plant a kiss on her cheek.

"Thank you for coming," he said, his voice husky in her ear. "In fact, thank you for messaging me. I was worried you might be put off by my silly title."

Though Mindy refused to admit as much to her aunt, she would not have called had it not been for the police requesting she do so. The concept of class mostly went over her head. Aunt Felicity dealt with rich, influential people every day, which meant Mindy did too. They were, almost exclusively, just like everyone else. They just had more money. Eddie though, was something else, and while she quite fancied dating the handsome man, the idea of mingling with royalty terrified her
.

Fighting against the feeling of being overwhelmed, Mindy focused on the dog.

"Who's this little fellow? Is he yours?"

"This is Henkel," Lord Chamberlain introduced his dog. "He's my partner in crime."

Mindy thought it was an odd choice of words and wondered if she'd just heard him admit the truth.

Lord Chamberlain offered his arm for her to hold – another thing she had never done before, yet which felt right in the circumstances – and they walked a few yards to the front entrance of Claridge's.

Tending the door, a man in top hat and tails recognised the man approaching and held the door open.

"Lord Chamberlain," he acknowledged as they passed him.

Beyond the doors, the entrance lobby was like something from a movie. At least, that's how Mindy's brain labelled it. The décor and abundance of marble together with everyone in sight dressed as though they were about to attend a ball hit the teenager's eyes in a wave of splendour so refined and overwhelming, she almost sprinted back outside to get some air.

Sensing his lunch date's hand stiffening, Lord Chamberlain, leaned his head down to whisper, "Don't worry, they're all feeling awkward too. We're just getting some lunch. It's nothing special."

Nothing special? The words echoed inside Mindy's head.

Expected by the maître d', they were led to a table in a corner where they could look out over the room but had no one behind them – a prime spot, Mindy observed.

"I've ordered us afternoon tea for two. I hope that's acceptable."

Mindy was hungry, but doubted this was the kind of place where she could order a fat sandwich with the fries inside.

She needn't have worried, for the afternoon tea, while elegantly presented, was plentiful. Little finger sandwiches with smoked salmon and cucumber, or ham with mustard had been cut so they were all the exact same size. Tiny cakes, each a mouthful of delight, were replenished each time they emptied the three-tiered platter set in the centre of the table and when they were done with that, a third course of food arrived – warm fruit scones served with clotted cream and jam.

By the time she started on those, Mindy was already beginning to worry she might be sporting a food baby in her snug dress.

There hadn't been much conversation so far which is to say Mindy was managing to mumble answers but was yet to introduce a topic of her own. There was one very simple reason for this: the police and her auntie wanted her to find out if Eddie – gorgeous hunk that he is – might be a jewel thief and a murderer. How was she supposed to bring that topic up?

Okay, so she could plant a bug in his room; that would be easy enough, so long as he was okay with her accompanying him back to the palace – she was going to use the excuse that her auntie would be there and that was how she was getting home – but what then? Could she figure out how to ask about the sapphire without tipping her hand?

If he wasn't involved in either crime, and surely that had to be the case, then she was going to be quite happy dating him for however long they could make it last. Heck, maybe this was her ticket to the high life.

With a mental shake of her head, Mindy shoved any such thoughts from her mind. She wasn't viewing Eddie as husband material just because he would be a duke one day.

Selecting a second scone so she had something for her mouth to do other than talk, Mindy continued to wonder how she was going to prove Eddie had nothing to do with the missing sapphire.

FeLICITY AT THE PALACE

At the palace, we were checked in again and instructed where to park. DI Munroe appeared, Amber's kitty carrier in her right hand. For a moment, my heart soared, thinking Amber was secured inside.

She wasn't though.

"She's been spotted twice in the last couple of hours," DI Munroe told us. "However, she runs the moment anyone goes near her and there are plenty of hiding places in the palace. It could be days before we catch her." Turning her gaze on Vince, she handed me the carrier and put out her hand for him to shake. "Detective Inspector Munroe."

"Vince Slater," he replied.

"*I'm Buster,*" said Buster, "*but we met yesterday so I guess you already knew that.*"

I jumped in quick before Vince could ruin things.

"Vince is my boyfriend," I announced, causing Vince's head to snap around so fast I though he must have left his eyeballs behind. "He's here to help me look for Amber. That's okay, isn't it?"

"*Oh, do we really have to?*" whined Buster.

DI Munroe nodded her head toward the door leading inside. "Follow me, please."

Stopping in her little office, she instructed Vince to remain outside and closed the door.

"Where is your niece, Mrs Philips? How do you propose to uphold your end of the bargain if she is not here?"

Trying to keep the smug from my face, I said, "She's having lunch in Claridge's with Lord Chamberlain as we speak."

DI Munroe failed to hide that she was impressed, and said, "That's fast work. Of course, it's not what we discussed. She needs to deploy the listening device somewhere in his rooms."

"I'm sure she'll get to that." The detective inspector and I were on very different missions. I felt a need to help Edward Smallbridge. I was less than convinced Lord Chamberlain had the sapphire, but that was why I had Vince with me – he could figure out who did what. I couldn't tell DI Munroe what he did though. He is a sneaky private investigator who opens doors like magic and deals with danger like it is an occupational hazard.

In the car on the way up, I had told him everything I knew – Edward's claim it had to be Lord Chamberlain because he was the only one in the back rooms at the right time and that I'd seen footage to confirm he was there that day.

Vince asked a few questions, most of which I couldn't answer, and fell silent to contemplate what he could do to prove the case one way or the other.

DI Munroe said, "I hope so, Mrs Philips. You trod a dangerous path last night in forcing my hand. Now you need to succeed." It sounded a lot like a threat. "Are you still investigating the possibility that Lord Chamberlain stole from Mr Smallbridge's jewellery shop?"

I said, "I am. Perhaps the two things are connected?"

DI Munroe's brow creased. "How would murdering his brother with a bespoke flight suit have anything to do with the theft of a sapphire?"

Ok, she had me there. I only said it because I wanted to have a reason for my plans to snoop.

Buster nudged my leg. "*Ask her where the bespoke flight suit came from. I could do with one of those.*"

With a shrug, and doing my best to ignore the dog's voice in my head, I ventured, "To help pay for things so they won't show up as transactions?"

Munroe considered that for a second, conceding, "You might have something there. Go look for your cat, Mrs Philips. If your niece is able to get herself invited into Lord Chamberlain's rooms, maybe you can have her look for your sapphire. I don't advise it though. Snooping where one ought not to ... let's say inside Lord Chamberlain's quarters, would be considered a crime akin to breaking and entering. But this is Buckingham Palace so the severity of the crime would be considered tenfold that of being caught in a commoner's house. It is the reason why I have not set foot inside his rooms and why your niece presents our best opportunity. If she is invited inside, she should place the device she was given and nothing more."

She looked down for a moment, considering something before continuing.

"As for Mr Smallbridge and the sapphire, I said I would give you two days and I will. Tomorrow night when that time is up, I will be speaking to Mr Smallbridge myself. The police will find the person behind the theft. I just pray the trail has not gone cold by then."

Sent on my way, I collected Vince and told him to shush as I hurried him away. My heart tapped out a staccato beat from the thoughts swirling in my head. DI Munroe made it very clear going into Lord Chamberlain's quarters was a bad thing to do. Nevertheless, I could see no other way to speedily release myself from Edward's obligation. If Vince found the sapphire, or some evidence of it – like he was trying to sell it on eBay – then my obligation to help Edward would be satisfied. It was risky, but I've seen Vince in action and felt confident he could pull this off.

Additionally, I knew Lord Chamberlain was out and unlikely to return for an hour or more – a lunch date is not something a person rushes. Furthermore, I wasn't happy that Mindy was tasked with deploying a bug in Lord Chamberlain's rooms. If we could pull this off (by we, I meant Vince) I could alleviate her of that burden.

Vince let me get him around the corner, where he pulled to a stop and said, "So 'girlfriend' what's the plan?"

Slumping my shoulders, I said, "I had to tell her you are my boyfriend. I'm not sure what you'll be able to do here, but I can't let her know I brought along a private security expert."

"Why not?"

"Because this is Buckingham Palace, dummy. No one is allowed to snoop here. There's no taking pictures, no going places you are not supposed to go ..."

"So how is it that we are walking freely through the ground floor?"

"Ah, well that's just an illusion." I came to the short flight of stairs that led to the tradespersons' reception desk. There had been nowhere to turn off in the short passageway connecting the two.

Sir Cuthbert was absent, a different man in his place.

"Mrs Philips," he greeted me, somehow aware of who I was. It made me wonder if my photograph had been circulated. "My name is Karson. DI Munroe let me know to expect you. And this is ..."

"Vince Slater," Vince extended his hand, squeezing the younger man's with his bone-crushing grip. "I'm her lover," he added, just to make me squirm.

I could have denied it was true, but doing so would just draw more attention.

Karson's eyes flared just a little, but I imagined he'd heard worse. Lifting the same small bell Sir Cuthbert used the previous day, he jingled it and set it down again just before the sound of approaching footsteps reached my ears.

Carrow appeared, popping into sight from around the corner much as he had last time.

"Mrs Philips," he nodded his head.

Karson didn't bother to look at the junior member of palace staff. "Carrow, Mrs Philips is here with Mr Slater to find her cat. I believe it went missing yesterday when you were supposed to be in attendance. Escort them now and help them to find the missing animal. Do not wander off this time."

His cheeks burning, Carrow dipped his head and backed away so we would follow.

Once we were out of Karson's earshot, Carrow slowed and turned. "Okay, Mrs Philips, where do you want to look first? There's a lot of palace to cover."

This is where it came in handy that I got to do a little snooping yesterday. I *was* here to find Amber, though if I'm being honest, I doubted she would let me catch her until she was ready. That was why I asked Carrow to take us to the Oxford Library. It was where I lost her yesterday, but more importantly, not far from Lord Chamberlain's quarters.

It was only now, when we were following Carrow through the palace that I began to question what it was that I hoped to achieve. I had Vince with me which was all very comforting because when it came to investigating, I had no idea where to start - I might have mentioned that already.

Where would Vince start though? He couldn't get into Lord Chamberlain's quarters. Or could he? Now that I thought about it, Vince was a magician when it came to locked doors. He knew his way around a computer better than your average nerd, and I would not be surprised if he could crack a safe. One day I was going to find out what lay in his murky past. For now, I needed to help steer him in the right direction.

With a basic understanding of the palace layout – this section was a big box around a courtyard – I asked if we could go right when we reached the top of a staircase.

Ahead of us, Carrow paused. "The Oxford Library is this way, Mrs Philips."

"Yes, but I doubt Amber is there waiting for me. Perhaps a circuitous route will allow us to cover more ground."

I went through the rigmarole of calling for Amber, all the while hoping I wouldn't find her just yet. If Vince was going to snoop, he would need to do it while Lord Chamberlain was at lunch with Mindy.

"Amber? Amber? Come on, sweetie. Come to mummy. There's a good cat."

Vince joined in. "Amber? Come on, kitty. Save us some time and make yourself visible."

Buster had his own thoughts on the matter. "*Amber, please stay lost in the palace. No one wants you at home. Especially not me.*"

I aimed a glare at the top of Buster's head, but refrained from comment.

After a minute, the pressure of listening to me and Vince calling for my cat got to Carrow and he joined in too. Now there were four of us calling for her if one cared to include Buster. Not that it made any difference.

I did my best to orientate myself as we came through the palace and mercifully was able to spot the door to Lord Chamberlain's rooms when we drew close to it. Nudging Vince, I pointed out what I was looking at.

"If he's got the sapphire, it will be in there," I hissed quietly so Carrow wouldn't hear.

Vince cocked an eyebrow. "You want me to break into a room inside Buckingham Palace and toss it looking for a missing sapphire?"

Automatically, I said, "No."

The dubious look on his face deepened.

"Okay, well sort of. But only if you think you can get away with it. I know the occupant isn't there because he's having lunch with Mindy."

I guess I'd left that part out because Vince blinked and smacked a hand against his ear as if to clear it. "I'm sorry. Your niece is out with a member of the royal household? I know she is smoking hot, but that's still ... surprising," he struggled to find a word that would fit.

"She is not smoking hot," I argued, though to be honest, I cannot deny that my niece is more attractive than I ever was at her age and she had a toned, healthy body that could grace a fitness magazine cover. "Anyway, she met him about ten yards from where we are standing now and he was very forward with her."

We were approaching the Oxford Library having gone around three sides of the square and I needed to distract Carrow if Vince was to achieve anything sneaky today.

"Oh, you need the restroom, dear?" I spoke loudly, pretending to respond to something Vince had said. "Upset tummy again? There are facilities just back there," I pointed where he needed to go which was going to take him back the way we had just come. "Catch up when you are done. Carrow and I will continue the search."

Vince narrowed his eyes at me, but said, "Thank you, dear. I shall try not to be too long."

Buster volunteered to go with him. "*Is this the dangerous part? Devil Dog is ready. Strictly speaking it ought to be night time if the dark shadow dwelling within my soul is going to fight crime, but the eerily quiet palace ambience goes some way to make up for the daylight."*

I wanted to tell him he was waffling a lot of nonsense, but Buster actually had a point. This *was* the time for him to go with Vince. His nose could separate out human smells from one another. If Vince got him inside Lord Chamberlain's rooms, maybe Buster would be able to confirm the same person was in Edward's private workshop yesterday.

Handing Buster's lead to Vince, I said, "Here, can you keep him with you, please? He's as likely to scare Amber off as he is to help us find her."

Buying Vince and Buster a window of opportunity, all I had to do now was keep Carrow occupied, and hope Vince could pull off the impossible by finding the jewel.

BY ROYAL APPOINTMENT

M indy pushed her plate away lest she be tempted to put anything else on it. Her imagined light lunch sat heavy while the
last remaining fruit scone taunted her from the top tier of the serving
platter.

Eddie chuckled at her. "You have a surprisingly good appetite."

Mindy felt her cheeks redden. Eddie was probably close to fifty percent
heavier than her, but had eaten only about half as much food. The
remains of her feast were evident in the trail of crumbs around her
place setting and the one big blob of strawberry jam staining the
otherwise pristine white tablecloth.

Attempting to shrug it off, Mindy said, "I work out a lot."

Eddie nodded and looked at her appraisingly. "That is evident."

To her surprise, when he looked at her, his eyes didn't linger where other guys' eyes might. He was looking at her arms and shoulders, meeting her eyes and rarely allowing his gaze to stray south. Like a voice echoing inside her head, she found a word to describe him: he was a gentleman.

It were as though someone had taken him to one side and trained him how to act and speak. He was unlike any of the other boys she had ever dated. She fancied him the first moment her eyes locked on his dazzling smile. Now, every minute she spent with him placed her further and further under his spell.

"Would you like to get a drink at the bar, or shall we vacate these premises and walk off our luncheon?"

Mindy didn't need to think about her answer. "A walk. Definitely a walk." She reached for her handbag to find her purse, only to find Eddie's hand touching her left forearm.

"If you will allow me, Mindy. This is my treat. I wasn't sure you would even message me and when you agreed to meet me for lunch, I paid in advance. I'm not trying to do the masculine 'let me pay' thing. You can get the next one if you wish. Is that acceptable?"

Mindy was used to paying half and she had her own money. Not a huge amount of it when compared to the son of a duke who lived in Buckingham Palace, but enough to pay her own way. Regardless, she was happy to duck the undoubtedly fat bill for their lunch at the insanely posh hotel, and it felt nice to be taken care of for once.

Outside in the street, with Henkel leading the way, she looped her hand back into the crook of Eddie's elbow and found she was biting her lip with indecision. She felt like kissing him. In fact, she felt the urge to kiss him more than she had ever experienced with any man in her short life to date.

Should she just do it? Now? In Oxford Street with people going by? She didn't give two stuffs about the opinion of the general public; it was how Eddie might react that plagued her mind. Well, that and the small yet worrying possibility he was a thief and a murderer.

Strolling among the shoppers coming in and out of the high-end London boutiques, Eddie chattered aimlessly about how he'd been forced by upbringing and parental expectations to join the army – he'd served as an officer in the Coldstream Guards for six years before his father considered his obligation to the family heritage complete.

Mindy, as she had been since she met him, was trying to find something to say when her eyes caught on the name of the next shop they were about to pass: Smallbridge Jewels and Timepieces by Royal Appointment.

Thinking fast, she said, "Ooh, can we go in here?" In her mind, if he was guilty of snatching the sapphire, Eddie would squirm and refuse. Or he would try to play it cool and accompany her inside where she could carefully frame a few questions that would expose his lies or confirm he was innocent.

Without replying, Eddie aimed his feet toward the door to jewellers.

"Of course. Looking to buy yourself a crown?" he joked. "I was here myself a couple of days ago. Smallbridge's have been taking care of the royal family for generations. They are the ones most likely to be approached by, let's say the king, if he wanted a special piece commissioned. I think they are currently looking after some of the jewels that will be worn for the coronation."

"Oh, I know," said Mindy, pleased to be up to speed on information for once. "Mr Smallbridge works with my aunt all the time. He was at my house last night."

Eddie's eyebrows climbed his head. "You don't say." Changing to a broad smile, he added, "There, you see? Our worlds are not so far apart."

Holding the door open with one arm, he escorted Mindy inside where they passed two burly security guards positioned either side of the entrance. Three members of staff were busy dealing with customers at the counters. A fourth member, a lady in her late thirties, smiled their way and said, "Good afternoon, Lord Chamberlain."

Mindy said, "Hello, Rhonda."

"And, oh, Mindy." Rhonda was so surprised to see Mindy very clearly with Lord Chamberlain that she blurted the words before she could stop them. Red now crimson, she managed to say, "Is there something specific I can help you with?"

It was at this point that Mindy recognised her need to have thought things through a little more carefully. She wanted to ask clever questions about the missing sapphire but how could she do that without mentioning that it was missing? Mr Smallbridge had been very specific about the need for total secrecy.

When an answer presented itself, she could barely get the words out fast enough.

"You know, I heard you have some of the pieces of jewellery for the coronation tucked away back there," with her head she indicated the door leading to the back rooms. "Is there any chance we can see them?"

Mindy posed the question to Rhonda but kept her hand looped into Eddie's elbow so she would feel it if he tensed. Glancing up at his face, he was as calm as they come. If he was a jewel thief, he was the coolest one in the world, and it made Mindy kinda hope he *had* stolen the sapphire.

Rhonda begged a moment to check with someone – a supervisor perhaps, Mindy didn't know all the relationships – but returned a moment later to invite them to follow her.

The one thing echoing in Mindy's head at that moment was that royalty get treated different. The other customers in the shop were glancing their way as Rhonda led them through the door to the back area.

They were going to see the tiara with the big hole where the sapphire was supposed to be. Mindy believed all she needed to do was ask one clever question about how it was missing. She wasn't going to ask Rhonda. Oh, no, her question would be aimed at Eddie.

How he reacted would end the game, but now she couldn't decide if she wanted him to be innocent, as she felt certain he must be, or some kind of debonair gentleman thief. The latter was distinctly more dangerous and thus much sexier.

All she had to do now was wait for the right moment.

cat calls

"Amber?" I continued to call for my cat and was no longer hoping she would take her time to appear. Twenty-four hours was quite long enough for us to be separated, thank you very much.

"Amber?" called Carrow, looking behind the curtains in the Oxford Library where I told him she might be hiding. "Won't she come when she's called?"

I shook my head and almost laughed at the idea.

"Clearly, you've never owned a cat."

Carrow looked my way. "No. I see them on TV adverts though. They come when someone opens their tin of cat food."

Opening my mouth to tell him that was the only time a cat might come, I groaned, slapped my forehead and cursed silently. Why hadn't

I thought to bring some of Amber's favourite food with me? The smell from a bowl of poached mackerel would have brought her back to me a lot faster than calling her name. In fact, I probably could have set an elaborate trap to catch her while I got on with something more pressing.

"Carrow, you are a genius."

Poor Carrow had no idea what he'd done to earn such praise.

"Could you be a sweetie and fetch a small bowl of food from the kitchens. Fish of some kind is her favourite. Mackerel if at all possible, but anything will do. I believe we can make her come to us."

Carrow's feet twitched.

"Um, well, I'm not really supposed to leave you alone in the palace," he replied though his voice lacked conviction.

"Oh, it will be fine. I'll stay right here," I lied, sitting in one of the chairs and taking a book from the shelf next to me. "Mr Slater will be along in a minute. We'll both wait here for your return." When he didn't move, I made encouraging shooing motions. "Go on, we're too old to get up to any mischief."

Still looking a little reluctant because he knew it was against protocol, Carrow nevertheless followed my suggestion.

I gave it a full minute before I left my chair and even then I tiptoed to the door to look around the frame. The coast was clear. How long would it take Carrow to get to the kitchen and back? Ten minutes? Less? More?

Given his reluctance to disobey the rules, I felt sure he would hurry. That should still afford me enough time to check on Vince though.

Hurrying to get there, I set off to make sure Vince was already in Lord Chamberlain's accommodation.

DECEPTION

"They were that brazen about it?" DI Munroe shook her head in disbelief.

"They were. First they pretended like Mr Slater needed to use the toilets. Then Mrs Philips came up with a genius plan to send me to fetch some fish from the kitchens. I resisted of course; didn't want to make it look suspicious when I agreed to leave her alone up there." Sitting on the table, Carrow propped one foot on a chair and dug a finger into the collar around his throat. "These things are sooo uncomfortable, Ma'am."

DI Munroe watched a monitor, her mind barely registering that Constable Carrow had spoken.

"That's undercover work for you, Carrow," she murmured. "Enjoy it while it lasts. You'll be back in uniform before you know it."

DI Munroe worried that might prove to be true rather sooner than she wanted. Her boss continued to breathe down her neck. She'd needed to stamp her foot to get her the undercover officer she needed to act as a plant inside the palace and even then they sent her a raw recruit not six months out of training.

They heard her when she raised her suspicions about Nugent Chamberlain's death and no one argued with her reasoning when they saw the evidence. They wouldn't touch the case though. Not when it involved a member of the royal family. To a man – and they were all men – they were all too concerned about their pensions to stick their necks out. So they let DI Munroe stick hers out instead.

Had she not been stupid enough to sleep with her married boss, the man who went on to be the head of the Metropolitan Police, she might have more leverage. As it was, she was lucky to still have a job.

That hung in the balance though. She needed to come up with something to prove Eddie Chamberlain was behind his brother's death. If she could pull that off, she would be too well known and respected for her boss to sack or dismiss her to some forgotten post. The flip side, obviously, was that failing to do so would give him all the ammo he needed to kick her out. Worse yet, if she were to get caught in the act of spying on Lord Chamberlain ... well, it would probably mean jail time.

That was why she duped poor Felicity Philips into believing there was a reason to help her. Discovering the wedding planner's relationship with a private investigator and that they had solved a few cases together was nothing more than serendipity playing into her hands.

She was vaguely aware the woman's recent weddings had gone awry with more than one murder occurring – DI Munroe had to perform background and security checks on the candidates nominated to manage Prince Marcus's wedding.

Hoping Felicity Philips might be daft enough to bring her security expert boyfriend into the palace and have him break into Lord Chamberlain's rooms was a longshot. Until she mentioned a missing sapphire that is.

It took her best acting to pretend she was going to give Edward Smallbridge two days before she approached him about the jewel theft. She couldn't give a stuff about it. If no crime had been reported, she was happy to act as though no crime had occurred.

The missing jewel made it even more likely they would illegally enter Lord Chamberlain's rooms and that would give her ample reason to go in there herself. In the ensuing chaos – DI Munroe intended to ensure there was plenty of it – she would have the chance to toss Lord Chamberlain's quarters and check there was nothing missing - a convenient excuse to cover her invasive search.

It pained her to have also deceived Jane Butterworth. The Blue Moon Detective was genuinely invested in bringing down the person behind the 'dragon'. It was kind of what she did. But how was DI Munroe to know Felicity Philips would blurt out the piece about the Heart of Windsor jewel? Until that moment, using Mindy to get a bug into Lord Chamberlain's room was the best plan they had.

They would 'discover' she had done it and as part of Mindy's arrest – later to be released without charge, of course – they would have cause to search Lord Chamberlain's quarters. I mean, what else might the lovesick teenager have done?

Butterflies in her stomach, DI Munroe watched the monitor. A camera positioned across the courtyard, filmed through the window of Lord Chamberlain's living space where Vince Slater moved stealthily from one area to the next.

All she had to do was wait and see what they turned up. Maybe there really was a sapphire to find. Who could tell? Perfect if there was. However, if not, she would spring her trap and arrest both Mrs Philips and her boyfriend. By the time Lord Chamberlain returned to the palace, his rooms would be crawling with the police and anything there was to find would be in her possession.

It was a perfect plan.

Until someone changed the game, that is. Right before her eyes, and in the space between heartbeats, her plan went out the window.

serious trouble

"Felicity what are you doing here?" Vince rolled his eyes and stepped back from the door to let me in.

"I'm checking on you," I replied, thinking that was obvious. "How did you get in?"

"Trade secrets. Here put these on and try not to touch anything." He handed me a pair of thin rubber gloves. "I've been through half the room. There is a safe, but I doubt I have time to open it. It makes sense that a priceless jewel would be in there rather than anywhere else, but honestly, what kind of idiot would bring it back to his accommodation? If I stole a giant sapphire, home would be the last place I'd take it."

Spotting the thing that was out of place or, in this case, missing, I asked, "Where's Buster?"

Vince knelt on the carpet to check the bottom drawer of an ottoman. "I couldn't bring him with me, could I? He'd leave fur everywhere and some might think of that as evidence of trespass. I've got to tell you, Felicity, this is not doing my heart any good. I don't mind getting into a few dodgy situations, but breaking and entering inside Buckingham Palace is a bit beyond me."

"So where is Buster?" I pressed for an answer, worried now that I had not one but two pets loose in the palace.

"I left him in the gents' down the hallway. He'll be fine for a few minutes."

I was about to say something else when movement caught the corner of my eye. Across the courtyard, soldiers were running. Not just running; they were sprinting. And they were armed.

Carrying their automatic rifles, their boots kicked up little puffs of dust. A startled member of palace staff watched them go, her eyes tracking their passage.

The feeling of dread now forming in my gut, doubled when I looked up to see more soldiers running past the windows on the other side of the courtyard. Unlike the ones I spotted first, these were already on our floor and there was little doubt left in my mind they were coming our way.

Unable to take my eyes from the worrying sight of armed servicemen coming my way, I reached out to grab Vince's arm. Squeezing it hard got his attention.

"What?" he asked, a little impatience in his tone.

"We need to leave."

"Amen to that."

"No," I tugged his arm to drag him along. "We need to leave right now!" I wasn't able to yank him to his feet; he probably weighed more than two of me, but he bounced up off his knees and needed only a half second to see what had me so flustered.

We were out the door two seconds later and angling left to get away from the onrushing sound of running boots.

"What about Buster?" I hissed, my heartrate through the roof.

Vince grabbed my hand and ran, taking me with him. "Buster will be fine! He can't get out. If we manage to avoid getting shot or arrested, we'll go back for him later!" I'd never heard Vince sound worried before and the tremor in his voice amplified my anxiety tenfold.

We passed the Oxford Library, Vince checking over his shoulder to see when the soldiers came into sight.

"How did they know?" he hissed. "There's no alarm on that door. I checked."

I had no answer to give, and my breathing was becoming ragged both from exertion as we ran and the adrenaline coursing through my veins.

"The stairs, Vince!" I shot an arm out to show where we needed to go. "There's a staircase on the right. That will take us down to the first floor."

"That'll do. We can pretend we were never up here."

"Make ready!" a gruff voice shouted. "Safeties on! No one shoots unless I give the order!" It came from the stairwell!

Vince said, "Change of plan!" and stopped abruptly, pulling me into his body to halt my forward momentum. I didn't need to ask what he was doing – we had armed soldiers coming from both directions and were about to be trapped like rats – Vince was opening a door.

He had tools in both hands; where they came from I didn't see, but he was crouched, down on one knee as he fiddled with the lock.

"They're coming," I gasped, urgency driving me to state what Vince already knew. "Hurry."

Vince's hands stopped moving and he swung his head around to look up at me.

"What do I get if I open the door?" he asked, his shark-infested smile back.

"What?" I couldn't believe he was stalling. "They're coming, Vince! Get the door open!"

"Only," he continued, "I cannot help thinking Buckingham Palace would be a heck of a place to consummate our relationship."

"What!"

"Since you're telling everyone I'm your boyfriend now."

I was going to punch him in the side of his head, but with a double pump of his eyebrows, he moved his hands and the lock opened. Before I could say anything further, he grabbed my hand again and yanked me through the door.

We were in another living area, high windows looking out over London this time as we were on the outside of the palace.

Vince got the door closed, doing so ever so carefully and quietly a second before the soldiers charging up the stairs reached the landing. A moment later they ran past the door.

Feeling like I hadn't drawn breath in the last thirty seconds, I gasped a ragged lungful and felt my head swim.

"Whoa there," Vince got an arm around me thinking I was about to collapse. "It won't be in our best interest to stay here. When they find Lord Chamberlain's quarters empty, they will expand their search."

Content I wasn't about to faint, Vince went to the door. Opening it just a crack, he looked out.

"How did they know?" I asked.

Vince's jaw was set with a grim smile when he flicked his head around to look at me.

"Someone tipped them off. That would be my guess." Closing the door again, Vince advanced on me, a worrying sparkle in his eyes. "Now, I don't want you to panic, but one alternative to running is to allow ourselves to be caught doing something else."

"You've got to be kidding." I already felt certain he wasn't.

He lifted his hands to make a sign that I shouldn't get agitated. "Think about it. The soldiers burst in and find us in a compromising position. It will explain why we are out of breath and a little sweaty and we can pretend like we have been in here the whole time."

He was actually serious.

When he came a step closer, I slapped at his hands. "Get away from me, Vince. I am not having sex with you in the palace!"

He sniggered. "Can't blame a guy for trying."

All humour halted the instant we heard someone opening the door.

DEVIL DOG

L istening through the restroom door, his head pressed to the floor so he could sniff the air outside, Buster tried to work out what was going on.

There were lots of people suddenly, all of them men if his nose was reading it right.

He got off his belly and tried to think. Should he bark to be let out? Vince led him in here by making it sound like it was somewhere they needed to go. The moment Buster went ahead to scope for danger in his Devil Dog mode, Vince told him to be a 'good boy' and shut the door.

"*Good boy*," rasped Devil Dog. "*Devil Dog isn't a good boy, he's the embodiment of vengeance and justice, a dark shadow hanging over the souls of those who would do evil, a curse criminals whisper about when they know their time is up.*"

Regardless of what Devil Dog might or might not be, he couldn't get the stupid door open. It wasn't even locked. If he nudged it with his head, it moved a little, swinging inward just a touch, but not enough for him to curl a paw around.

Beyond the door, the men outside were shouting and agitated. It sounded like they were looking for something or someone. Buster listened and sniffed, catching the scents of boot polish and a mix of various aftershaves and body sprays combined with sweat.

None of that told him anything worthwhile. He needed to get out. Felicity was out there somewhere and was bound to need his help; she always did. She had Vince, and he was helpful for a human, but hardly the same thing as having a bona fide superhero to offer protection.

A man's voice commanded, "Check the rooms! He must be hiding somewhere; there's no way he got past us. Remember, he's a man in his late fifties, wearing a grey suit. Arrest and detain. Only fire if you believe your life is in danger."

They were coming room by room? Buster backed up a step, setting his paws so they were ready to propel him through the restroom door the moment it opened.

More shouts echoed outside, the men opening doors and clearing rooms as they swept along the hallway.

Buster saw a shadow fall outside; two pairs of boots on the carpet right by the door a moment before it burst open. If he'd been closer, it would have flattened his nose.

Springing forward, Buster made a break for it. He didn't know who these chaps were, but he recognised a gun when he saw one.

The first man yelled in startled surprise. There was a large hairy blob coming his way at speed and it filled him with momentary terror. The man behind him would have laughed at his colleague's girly squeal were it not for the fact that Buster ran right through his legs. Not between them. Through them.

Floored when his boots went from beneath to behind him without warning, the soldier crashed down on top of his weapon. In the hallway, half a dozen of the palace guards whipped around to track the dog.

Two were in Buster's path. Not knowing which way to go, he'd chosen the path of least resistance – there were more soldiers in the other direction. Now he needed to avoid getting caught.

"It's a dog, Sir!" shouted one man.

The reply came just as Buster jinked around the hands flailing to stop him.

"I can see that, thank you, Jennings. I think we can assume he's not our invader." Captain Raef Duncan was desperate for action. Getting assigned to the palace was a prestigious role that would do his career no harm whatsoever. However, it was boring beyond belief. They were ceremonial guards, nothing more. Well, until something occurred and there was tangible threat to the royal family or the palace itself. Then, and only then, were they permitted to respond as a Quick Reaction Force.

An invader not only inside the palace but in the quarters of a member of the royal household, well that qualified for sure.

"Leave it," he commanded, when the soldiers blocking the dog's path failed to stop it.

Buster yanked his leg free of the human hand that almost caught him and ran for his life. In his wake, Captain Duncan fired off another command.

"Get back to the search! I want this man found. Someone is going to spend the next few years in a maximum-security jail."

unexpected saviour

My heart was in my mouth as the door began to swing inward. In a panic, I threw myself at Vince, hitching up my dress and lifting one leg so it would look like we were in a passionate embrace.

"No time for any of that," hissed Carrow, poking his head around the doorframe. Beckoning urgently, he said, "Come with me. Right now!"

I had no idea what was going on, but he appeared to want to help us escape our situation and I was not about to start arguing.

Carrow ducked his head back out to check the hallway was clear before beckoning again with even more urgent movements.

"Come on, hurry! They're coming!"

There was no need to convince us, and we were already moving, Vince making sure I was ahead and not getting left behind as I shuffled the bottom of my dress back into place.

Going out the door, Vince touched my shoulder and whispered, "Nice stockings. I might request you wear those again some time."

That he could remain so calm and still be so focused on his desire to get my clothes off made me gasp. I wanted to swat him with my hand but he was already moving out of range, catching up to Carrow who led us to the stairs. They were clear now; no soldiers positioned to catch us if we managed to avoid their search. It felt a little sloppy, but I was glad for it either way.

"Quickly," Carrow encouraged.

Following on and keeping pace, I paused to kick off my shoes – they were making too much noise and I feared they would give away our position.

"Where are we going?" Vince wanted to know.

"Somewhere safe." A cryptic answer if ever I heard one, but there was no time to quiz Carrow on specifics because we were spotted.

Passing a window on the south side of the square courtyard, soldiers one floor up and looking at us from the west side started yelling loud enough for us to hear them. One glance showed figures running again, whipping by the windows as they hurtled in our direction.

I doubted they could see clearly enough to know who they had seen, but the haste of our movements tipped them off and we were being pursued again.

I expected Carrow to panic and run, but instead, he slowed to a walk.

"This way," he said, turning to take a narrow passage that ran perpendicular to the one we were in. Instantly, we were in a new part of the palace; one I hadn't seen in my previous ventures. It skirted the outside of the giant building, a sharp left turn angling us back toward the entrance where we came in.

Was Carrow taking us back to Vince's car? Was the plan to escape the soldiers by sending us home? What about Buster and Amber?

CHanGInG ATTITUDes

Amber was becoming increasingly concerned about her well-being. There were corgis following her scent. They were not particularly bright which enabled her to avoid them twice when she climbed above their heads and got to watch them scamper by below.

They were persistent though.

Her dream of a new life in a palace with the handsome prince doting on her every need was just about shattered. She couldn't find him anywhere and had all but given up hope.

Maybe he wasn't even here. That would explain why he was so impossible to locate. It was all Buster's fault, of course. Amber hadn't fully figured out why the bulldog was to blame but he had to be – everything was his fault.

Dropping silently to the floor having avoided the corgis for the second time, she checked to be sure they were gone and set off in the opposite direction.

There were humans shouting about something, the sound coming from somewhere distant. It was of no concern to her. The only human she held any interest in was her prince. Although, she considered, he was proving to be a bit of a let down.

Swept off her paws by his debonair charm, he'd subsequently vanished, leaving her heartbroken and alone. Felicity had never done that.

Felicity had her faults; plenty of them, in fact. They started with letting the stupid bulldog into the house when he could survive adequately tied to a post in the garden. She never let Amber go hungry though, and was always there to comfort and praise her when she wanted human affection.

Wondering if perhaps she'd been too hasty in running away. Amber decided to return to the spot where she last saw her.

GeT ReaDy TO LIe

C arrow did not lead us out of the building, but turned right at the last moment just before we reached the exit. Suddenly, I realised where he was taking us: to DI Munroe! The deceitful git had tricked us! He was going to turn us over to the police officer in charge and claim the credit for apprehending us!

Spinning about in a panic, I bumped into Vince's broad chest and bounced off. I wanted to leave. We would run to his car and escape while we could. I wasn't entirely convinced we could get past the police barrier controlling traffic in and out, but it was better than meekly surrendering ourselves.

Where had it all gone wrong? Yesterday I was floating on clouds having just been awarded the contract to plan and manage the next royal wedding. Now I was thinking in terms of outrunning the law. It was making my head spin.

Edward.

His name resounded in my head. Edward had put me up to this.

"Going somewhere, Mrs Philips?" DI Munroe asked as I attempted to silently turn Vince around.

She was coming out of the ladies' restroom behind us, and we were caught between her and Carrow now. My heart sank yet again.

"Perhaps we should speak in my office." She made it sound like a polite suggestion though I felt certain it was anything but.

Trudging after Carrow and imagining this was how it must feel for a condemned person on their way to the gallows, I rallied my brain to find some way of explaining away our actions. She had to know we had broken into Lord Chamberlain's rooms. She had to know that was why the soldiers were after us. With a gasp, I realised it was probably DI Munroe who sent the armed men to catch us.

The moment we were inside her office, DI Munroe shut the door and started talking.

"Captain Duncan will be here soon. You will let me do the talking, is that understood?"

I glanced at Vince to see if he had any idea what was going on and got a shrug.

"He cannot know you were in Lord Chamberlain's quarters. No one can ever know. Are we clear on that?" DI Munroe waited for us to answer.

"I don't understand?" I mumbled. "What's going on?"

DI Munroe sucked in a deep breath and let it go slowly.

"Did you find the missing sapphire?"

"What?" Was I supposed to admit we were searching for it in Lord Chamberlain's rooms? Was this a clever ruse to get us to confess so she could arrest us?

"The missing sapphire, Mrs Philips? Did you find it in Lord Chamberlain's quarters? Hurry, please, we do not have much time."

Vince said, "No. I found nothing of worth."

"Were you able to access the safe? Was there anything in it?"

Again it was Vince who answered. "There was too little time." Frowning, he asked, "What were you hoping I would find. This isn't about a sapphire, is it?"

I said, "I'll tell you later."

DI Munroe shot back, "No, you will not, Mrs Philips. Official secrets, remember?"

"Oh, yeah."

Now it was Vince's turn to look at me with questioning eyes.

DI Munroe cut through our thoughts. "Look, Captain Duncan is on his way here right now because I questioned what he and his soldiers were doing running all over the palace with their weapons drawn. I don't know how he knew you were in Lord Chamberlain's room, but he clearly did. That is why we are going to deny the truth until we are blue in the face. You have been here talking to me ever since you arrived at the palace. You are here to collect your cat ..."

"And dog," I interjected quickly.

DI Munroe looked about, noticing for the first time that Buster wasn't with me.

"You lost the dog too?"

"But we know where he is," I replied, hoping that made things a little better. "He's in a restroom on the first floor not far from the Oxford Library."

The detective inspector exhaled sharply.

"You're waiting here for the palace staff to find your pets and bring them to you. Got that? You haven't been anywhere."

Vince and I recited our story. It was a simple one to remember at least.

When I glanced at Carrow, curious as to how he fitted into the equation, DI Munroe supplied an answer I was not expecting.

"Constable Carrow works for me. Good thing too or the pair of you would be in cuffs by now."

The sound of approaching voices and boots on the floor halted all further conversation. A sharp rap on the door – knuckles on wood, preceded Munroe opening it.

"Captain Duncan, I hope you have a good explanation."

ANONYMOUS TIP OFF

C aptain Duncan stood more than six feet tall which placed his head almost a foot above DI Munroe's. That did nothing to impact her control or superiority.

Her question, however, went unanswered because the captain spotted Vince and went nuts. Raising his weapon, he bellowed, "That's the man who broke into Lord Chamberlain's quarters! Seize him!"

The soldiers massing to his rear surged forward and might have flooded Munroe's small office had she not barked a counter command.

"Halt! All of you." She had grabbed the muzzle of Captain Duncan's rifle and was forcing it back down – though it took all her might to make it move an inch against the strength of the man holding it. "This man has not left my office since he arrived at the palace. What reason could you possibly have for thinking he invaded Lord Chamberlain's rooms?"

"She's right," said Vince, sounding casual and convincing. "Felicity and I were not permitted to wander as we hoped we might be. We've been here the whole time."

Captain Duncan was not about to be put off.

"We received a tip that a man matching his exact appearance was inside Lord Chamberlain's quarters. You expect me to believe that's pure coincidence?"

"Exact match, huh?" DI Munroe mocked his claim. "You have any idea how often the police get the wrong person? What did the tipster say? Grey suit, grey hair, well built ..."

Vince puffed out his chest with a sly grin in my direction.

I rolled my eyes.

"mid-fifties ... that could almost be a description for Sir Cuthbert." Softening her voice, DI Munroe said, "Raef, you just ran your entire troop around the palace reacting to a hoax call. I suggest you shut the door with your soldiers outside so your subordinates don't hear the rest of this conversation."

She had already won, that much was evident. A tinge of pink high-lighted the army officer's cheeks as he reached for the door and instructed his troops to wait outside.

"There was a dog in the restroom just along from Lord Chamberlain's quarters," he was trying to mount a defence and I honestly felt a little sorry for him.

"A dog?" DI Munroe's mocking tone continued. "Did you shoot it, Raef?" Before he could respond she said, "Look, I could probably have you fired from your job here before the sun sets. How would that impact your promotion prospects? You ran around the palace with your guns out, Raef. Did you even get a name from the person who left the call?" I noted she didn't question whether there had actually been one.

"No," he admitted. "It was anonymous."

"And it matched this man's description?"

"Yes," he nodded.

She shrugged. "Then I guess it was someone connected to Mr Slater playing a little trick."

"A little trick?" Captain Duncan scoffed. "I would hardly call this a little ..."

"What would you call it? I would call this whole situation a gross over-reaction. Soldiers running through the palace, kicking down doors ..."

"No one kicked down any doors." Captain Duncan continued to defend his actions despite being on the back foot.

DI Munroe continued as though Raef hadn't spoken. "Scaring the staff ... what if you had run into one of the royals? What if your Rambo wannabes startled Sir Cuthbert and gave him a heart attack? This never happens again, Captain Duncan. Do I make myself clear?" She waited for an answer.

213

Unwilling to bow down, Captain Duncan said, "You expect me to do what the next time there is a credible threat to the palace? Carry on as though nothing is happening? You know I can't do that."

"Do nothing? No, but you can contact me. Or one of the other police officers. You have a responsibility to respond as an armed force in the event that you are needed. You do not get to decide when that is. Now, are we clear on this, Captain Duncan or do I need to file a report?"

The threat of paperwork did the trick.

"We are clear," he spat through gritted teeth. With a final glare at Vince, he left the office, throwing the door shut behind him.

I gasped a breath, feeling like I'd been holding it for an hour.

DI Munroe slumped against the corner of a table. "Carrow, be a good chap and put the kettle on, won't you?"

I, for one, wanted something stronger than tea.

Forcing herself to move, Munroe crossed the room. "I think it would be best if you were to leave now, Mrs Philips. If you can avoid it, don't come back here for a few days. I know you have a wedding to plan, but perhaps you can make arrangements with the prince and Miss Morley by phone."

I could not agree more, but there was one rather pressing matter of business that still required my attention.

"What about Buster and Amber?"

On THE CAT'S TRAIL

B uster stopped at a large potted plant. Bouncing up onto his back paws, he placed his front paws on the rim of the pot and sniffed.

Amber had been here. In fact, Amber had chosen to use the potted plant as her outhouse. Wanting a better sniff, Buster dug in with his front claws for grip and pushed off with his back legs.

Unfortunately, designed by nature to look like a footstool with eyes and a tail at opposite ends, he was far from the most gymnastic of God's creatures. His back end came off the ground, his little legs scrambling in the air for purchase and that was where it all went wrong.

Feeling the pot topple, Buster released his grip and pushed away to get clear. The pot, the plant, and the dirt in which it sat crashed to the floor as he ran to get out of range. The topmost leaves swiped at his bottom, making him jump, but he escaped unscathed.

The nibbled remains of Amber's offering skittered and rolled across the floor to stop a foot from Buster's nose.

"*Definitely Amber*," he confirmed.

He'd been tracking her for half an hour, but her scent doubled back on itself repeatedly. Not only that, he could smell the corgis. Were they following her? Or were their scents here by coincidence? Buster couldn't tell, but leaving a mark on the wall – his thirty seventh since escaping the restroom – he trotted off to see if he could find her.

Anomaly

A cross town, in the back rooms of Smallbridge Jewels and Timepieces. Mindy was yet more convinced her new beau had nothing to do with the stolen sapphire. He didn't react at all when she asked about the royal jewels Smallbridge's held.

In fact, he seemed just as keen as her to see the pieces.

"I've seen most of them before at one point or another, but I'm pretty far removed from the actual crown, you realise. Were my papa not such a close friend of the King's, I might not have the place in Buck House."

"Buck House?"

Eddie chuckled. "Yes, my dear. That's what us insiders call the place. Buckingham Palace is too much of a mouthful." He fell silent for a moment, his eyes unfocused to give Mindy the impression he was running something through his head. "Say, if I'm not being too forward, would you like an escorted tour? Nothing inappropriate suggested, I assure you."

Mindy could not help a smile from spreading across her face; Eddie was so sweet. He was inviting her back to his place, and doing his best to promise he had nothing untoward in mind.

Mindy's own thoughts were a little darker, a little more carnal. If he whispered something naughty in her ear, she wasn't entirely sure how she would react. If he didn't, well maybe she would be the one doing the whispering.

Rhonda led them into the workshop where Mindy recognised Kitty and Alicia.

She waved. "Hi. Back again," she said, feeling filled up with joy by the day she was having.

The ladies smiled and waved before going back to their work.

Speaking quietly, and hoping she knew something Eddie didn't, Mindy said, "They are making pieces for the King to give to the Maharaja of Zangrabar. He's getting married."

Eddie gawped at her. "Firstly, how do you know the Maharaja is getting married? I didn't know that. When did it become public knowledge? Secondly, how do you know what they are working on?"

Mindy elbowed him in the gut playfully. "I told you I was here yesterday, silly. Mr Smallbridge told me what they were working on. I know about the marriage because I know Patricia Fisher and I was with her when she got her invitation."

Eddie shook his head from side to side. "I'll not pretend to know anything about you Mindy, but you are full of surprises. How do you know Patricia Fisher?" he asked as casually as he could manage. That his date, an attractive young lady he would soon convert to girlfriend status, knew a famous sleuth was a little disconcerting. He had big plans. Secret plans. Plans that included people dying. The last thing he needed was a loose cannon busybody sticking her nose where it wasn't wanted.

Mindy shrugged. "She's an old friend of my aunt. We just got back from organising a billionaire's wedding on board her cruise ship."

Ah, so she was still on the cruise ship. Not too much to worry about then.

Lord Chamberlain's thoughts were interrupted by Rhonda returning with several pieces of jewellery.

Paying attention to something other than Eddie for the first time since they arrived, Mindy found herself frowning. A memory had just surfaced.

"I thought these were all locked in Mr Smallbridge's private workshop?" That's what Mr Smallbridge said yesterday. He said he was the only one with access to them. Only now that she could see the same items he had in the workshop did she spot the anomaly.

Rhonda looked at her. So too did Kitty and Alicia.

"Private workshop?" questioned Rhonda. "We don't have one of those. Mr Smallbridge hasn't worked on any of the jewellery for years."

GLIMPSING THE TRUTH

Walking back through the palace hallways at a steady, sedate pace, we were once again prevented from leaving because of my pets. At least we knew where Buster was. Amber was another story.

I wanted to think about getting into Vince's car and putting this terrifying, embarrassing episode behind me. Never again would I allow myself to be sweettalked into playing the role of sleuth or spy or whatever the heck I had become in the last forty-eight hours.

My train of thought led me back to Edward. My old friend asked me to help him, and that was fine even if it was a massive imposition. That wasn't the part tickling my brain. It was his insistence I include Vince in my supposed investigation.

Someone had phoned in with a hoax call to tell Captain Duncan's men there was an intruder. It wasn't a hoax though. Vince really was inside Lord Chamberlain's quarters and how could anyone know that?

They gave an accurate description of Vince, right down to the colour of his suit, but there was no mention of me. It struck me as odd.

The more I thought about it, the more strange it all seemed. The caller not only knew the number to contact the palace guard force of soldiers they also knew precisely where to send them. How many people on the planet would even know they existed, let alone their number?

Captain Duncan said they were told to go to Lord Chamberlain's quarters. How could anyone know Vince was there unless they were watching. And if they were watching, why didn't they see me? There was no mention of a woman intruder, only Vince. Not only that, Vince tossed the room and found nothing incriminating. Okay, so the jewel could have been in the safe, but was it? Vince questioned why anyone would be stupid enough to bring it back to their home and he was right.

With a gasp, I questioned if maybe the caller did see me but chose not to mention my presence. A chill crept up my spine as I glimpsed the answer. My lips twitched, a sentence forming in my head when Vince let out a small grunt of pain and fell to the floor. Walking right by my side, I spasmed in fright to see the big man collapse by my feet.

At the sudden sound, Carrow spun around to see what was amiss and all I could do was squeal as someone barrelled through me. Knocked roughly to one side, I came to rest half on the floor, half against the wall.

Poor Carrow was also down, what looked like a halberd poking from his chest. Petrified and unable to get my voice to work, I looked up as the attacker turned his attention on me.

uncovering the truth

"What do you mean he's not here?" Mindy demanded, her voice rising even as she tried to stay calm. "He stated categorically that he would not be able to join my aunt at the palace today because he was needed here. He was going to be here all day." She heard everything Mr Smallbridge said when he was leaving her aunt's last night because her room is next to the front door.

Rhonda, a little taken aback by Mindy's forceful attitude, could only apologise.

"I'm sorry. I don't know what else to tell you. Mr Smallbridge has not been in all day. He is never here on a Sunday."

"And he doesn't have a private workshop where no one else is ever allowed to go?" Mindy sought to confirm for the third time.

Rhonda shook her head, the other ladies in the room backing her up.

"No. If he did, it would remain unused. I do not recall the last time he worked on a piece of jewellery himself. It's not what Mr Smallbridge does."

Mindy rubbed a hand against her forehead. This was all wrong. Mr Smallbridge wanted them to snoop around Eddie and find out what he had done with the priceless sapphire he stole. Mr Smallbridge said he was the only one who knew the door code to get into the workshop where the royal jewels were located.

Snapping her eyes back up to meet Rhonda's, she said, "Next you're going to tell me the Heart of Windsor isn't missing."

Thirty-eight seconds later Mindy exploded from the front door of the jewellers with Lord Chamberlain on her heels trying to keep up. She had her phone in her hand and was ignoring Eddie's questions as she tried to get through to her aunt.

"What's going on, Mindy?" Eddie puffed, running alongside her with Henkel tucked under one arm like a rugby ball, and starting to question his fitness for she showed no sign of even breathing yet. "What was all that about the sapphire? Where are we going?"

"Back to the palace!" she shouted. The phone went to voicemail, and she cursed. She placed the call in the vague hope her aunt might have it with her or that maybe she wasn't inside the palace yet. Trying Vince's phone brought the same result.

Stuffing it into her handbag, she shucked her shoes, abandoning them in the street so she could run barefoot.

A shout of, "Leave them!" deterred Eddie from stopping to fetch the shoes and she ran backwards for a few steps to make sure he was keeping up.

"You have numbers for the palace, right? A number for someone in the security detail?"

"Of course."

Mindy felt a momentary wave of relief. "Then call them. I think Edward Smallbridge is at the palace and if he is then he is up to something."

cornered

Amber slunk along the edge of a wall, keeping to the shadows. Her thoughts of finding the prince had long since been banished and she just wanted to go home. Finding her way out, however, was proving more than a little difficult.

The palace was a gigantic maze of crisscrossing corridors and enormous rooms. The Oxford Library, where Amber forlornly hoped she might find Felicity, was silent and empty just like most of the rest of the palace.

She had not seen the corgis for more than fifteen minutes which came as a relief, but too focused on finding a way out so she could begin to think about finding a way home, Amber sauntered around a corner to find her path blocked.

"*Hello, Kitty,*" said Sandy, a wolf's leer spread across his face.

Amber would laugh at a corgi and slap its silly face if it came near her. However, this was not one corgi, and the same thing could not be said when facing a pack.

"*Wandered into the wrong palace, did we?*" asked Misfit.

Amber took a pace backward, glancing to her right as some of the corgis on the periphery came forward and began to angle around to get behind her.

"*I'm looking for the way out. Show me the way and I'll leave,*" said Amber, making sure her voice sounded haughty and proud; the way a cat should sound.

It was a mistake.

"*Oh, you'll be leaving all right,*" snarled Muriel. "*In pieces!*"

With a squeal of fright, Amber turned tail and ran. She had no direction in mind, the point was to run. The corgis were giving chase and though they were not the most athletic of dogs, they were keeping pace, their snapping and yapping terrifying to Amber's ears.

Onward she ran, flying over the carpet with a whole pack of dogs on her tail. Up. She needed to go up! Why was there nothing to climb? Maybe she could climb the wall, but how long could she hold on for? What if she climbed a curtain and it fell? That happened once at Felicity's house when Buster chased her. She got all caught up in the material and the rotten bulldog widdled on her head.

The corgis would do much worse.

Running scared, she wished there were other cats at the palace. A swarm of cats would soon alter the statistics, but in all her searching she'd found not one trace of another feline.

"*Slow down, cat!*" barked Misfit. "*There's nowhere to go. Sooner or later we are going to catch you and when we do, we are going to rip you to shreds. Running is just making us angrier!*"

Beginning to tire, Amber wished she was back at home asleep on the sofa. She wouldn't mind if she had to share it with Buster. Anything was better than this.

"*Dun, dun, DAH!*"

The trumpet call of Buster's stupid alter ego was like a choir of angels to Amber's ears. The bulldog flew out of a cross corridor, piling through the lead corgis to scatter them like pins before a bowling ball.

Amber dared a look over her shoulder to see if Buster was all right and found he was already running after her.

"*It's that bulldog again!*" barked Muriel.

"*The one whose been leaving his mark all over the palace!*" joined Elton.

Candy squealed, "*Kill him too!*"

The dogs Buster floored hadn't stayed down for long. They were back on their feet and in pursuit but the gap between them was greater now.

"*What took you so long?*" mewled Amber.

Buster cocked an eyebrow. "*Good to see you too, cat. How about we find Felicity and get the heck out of here?*"

It was a suggestion she could get behind, so with a truce in place for now, Amber and Buster turned a corner and ran down a flight of stairs. It looked familiar to them both, but the chasing pack of corgis was still right on their tails.

ReVeaLInG THe TruTH

Rising slowly to my feet, I didn't dare take my eyes off the man glowering at me. He had a glob of spittle on his chin and his hair and suit were both skewwhiff from the effort of his attack.

"Edward?" I kept my hands where he could see them. "What are you doing? What have you done?" I glanced at Carrow; was he breathing? "Edward, I think you've killed him." I took a step in Carrow's direction.

"Leave him!" Edward bellowed. "Why would you care more about him than you do about me?"

Unable to make my brain process what was happening, I froze to the spot again when Edward reached down to pick up the small bronze bust he'd used to brain Vince.

"Care?" I repeated Edward's word. "He's hurt, Edward. You stabbed him."

Edward's features formed a mask of confusion for a second. "Not him!" he shouted, meaning Carrow. "To hell with him. He's just a lackey for the palace." He kicked Vince's inert form. "I'm talking about this oaf. Why would you pick him over me? Huh? What's he got that I haven't?"

Adrift on a sea of bewilderment, little dots began to join at the back of my head.

"Money? Ha!" Edward snapped. "I don't think so. Prestige? Standing in the community? None of those? Is he better looking? Better in bed? How would you know, Felicity, you never so much as kissed me."

"Edward, I don't understand," I wailed. "What is happening here?"

He hefted the bronze bust. "It's quite simple, Felicity. This oaf was supposed to get caught sneaking around inside Lord Chamberlain's quarters. The soldiers would have arrested him, the police would have charged him, and he would have been out the way. Yet somehow, none of that came to pass. The slippery," Edward paused to kick Vince again, "oaf found a way to escape. You are supposed to be mine, Felicity."

"The sapphire was never missing, was it?"

Edward squinted in misunderstanding. "What? Oh. No, of course it wasn't. Are you kidding me? With all the security around the place now I have the royal jewels in the building, it's a wonder I can get in and out myself. No one could steal so much as a gram of gold without getting caught."

"So why blame Lord Chamberlain?"

Edward gave me a look that suggested I was being particularly dense.

"Because he lives in the palace. Do you know how many members of the royal family live full time in Buckingham Palace?" He let the question hang for a second before answering it himself. "One. One, Felicity. I had to wait weeks for Lord Chamberlain to come to the shop so I could capture video evidence of him coming and going. I knew I would need something to make my story more convincing. And you bought it. You bought it all and I knew this oaf," he poked Vince with the toe of his shoe, "would be only too pleased to lend you his help. I have to say, Felicity, you must be dynamite in the bedroom for him to be this loyal."

I gasped again, offended by what he had said, but knew now was not the time to discuss the intricacies of my relationship with Vince. Edward did not look like he was of a mind to believe anything I said anyway.

Taking a step forward and clutching the bronze bust in both hands, Edward showed me an apologetic face. "Sorry, Felicity. I never expected it to come to this. But if I cannot have you, then no one can."

Oh, my God! He was going to kill me. Edward Smallbridge, a man I had known for thirty years, now planned to beat me to death in Buckingham Palace because he thought I was in love with Vince.

Maybe I was, but if it were the case, the depth of my feelings had only reached that state in the last few hours.

Edward could have wooed me if he'd tried. He hadn't though and his one fumbled attempt to take me to dinner ended when Vince showed up.

I had enough presence of mind to try to run. Unfortunately, I was looking at Edward and not where I was going. I tripped on Carrow's outstretched feet and fell, landing awkwardly on my front.

Rolling over to defend myself with my hands, I saw that Edward had frozen. He held the bust high above his head, ready to launch it at me and come in close and use it as a blunt object, but he wasn't moving.

"Do you hear that?" he asked, confused about something.

I almost apologised for having no idea what he was talking about. Thankfully, I came to my senses a heartbeat later, rolled onto my front again and scrambled to get my feet moving.

I was just coming into a sprinter's stance, arms pumping to get me going when the impossible sight of my cat and dog filled my vision.

They exploded into the hallway before me, coming off a wide staircase that led to the first floor. They were moving at an incredible rate as though they somehow knew I was in danger and were coming to save me.

Edward's shouts filled the air; he was chasing me!

Behind Amber and Buster, a pack of corgis appeared, the small dogs also coming from the stairwell. They were barking like mad and it looked to me as though they were chasing my pets.

The bronze bust struck my right shoulder, knocking me off balance and sending a cascade of pain through my body.

Flailing with my arms, I knew I was going to crash into the carpet. There was nothing I could do to stop it. Edward would be on me in an instant, but converting my fall into a dive, I got out of the way of my pets and shouted, "Save Felicity!"

Buster's Devil Dog voice appeared in my head, "*Dun, dun, DAH!*"

Edward said, "What the ..."

I twisted my head around to see and got to watch my attacker flip into the air. Buster had performed his usual trick of running right through Edward's legs. However the jeweller fared, he would not be running anywhere anytime soon. Buster had broken ankles using the same tactic in the past.

Amber kept running but only as far as Mindy who was tearing along the hallway with Lord Chamberlain on her heels. Behind him I could see DI Munroe checking Carrow's vitals.

Oblivious to the humans heading his way, Edward started to get to his feet only to be pummelled by a pack of corgis who ran right over the top of him.

I also started to get up, but made the mistake of using my right arm. Where it attached to my shoulder exploded in a kaleidoscope of pain that made my head spin.

Edward rose to his feet, his face locked in a grimace. He was angrier than a nest full of hornets and utterly focused on me. That was why he didn't see Mindy coming.

"Excuse me," she said politely.

Startled by her voice, Edward swung his head around to look and got a spinning foot uppercut to his chin. He collapsed like someone had flicked his switch to the off position.

Still holding Amber, Mindy knelt to check his pulse and called for DI Munroe to bring some cuffs.

If ever there was a time for gin, this was it.

Aftermath

L ord Chamberlain commanded the corgis to desist, and they obeyed immediately. He had Buster in his arms – not the easiest of feats – and had to wait for palace staff to arrive to round the corgis up before he could put him down. Henkel was on the floor, buzzing around the corgis to find out what was going on.

Carrow was in a bad way but looked likely to survive. The blade had penetrated his chest but missed his heart or he would have been dead already. As paramedics checked me over and declared Vince had a head like a piece of moonrock to have survived a blow that ought to have killed him, I found myself in Amber's company.

She came to me without being encouraged and curled on my lap where I sat on a chair one of the palace staff kindly provided.

"Are you coming home with me now?" I asked, giving her fur a stroke.

Her eyes closed as she leaned into my hand, Amber purred, *"Yes, I think I shall. Buster earned a few forgiveness points today."*

It was a typical cat answer: she didn't apologise for her behaviour and made it sound like she was willing to grace us with her presence even though we barely deserved it.

Mindy explained how she figured it out and that Eddie, as she insisted on calling him, was the sweetest, most wonderful man she'd ever met. She was smitten, that much was obvious.

Vince needed to go to hospital just as a precaution. I wanted to go with him, but he insisted I should go home. Nothing was broken, I was just bruised and would be stiff and sore for a few days. The paramedics were nevertheless borderline about taking me in too and only agreed to let me go because I had people at home to look after me.

Well, I had Mindy. My niece had received a text message from her mother at some point during the afternoon in which Ginny said she was back with her husband and had already collected her things from my house.

This was good news on multiple fronts. Mindy was in no hurry to return home where she said her parents were reaffirming their marriage. She was good enough to not expand on what she thought that meant.

With Vince's keys in my hand, I watched his ambulance leave the palace grounds. I would call and message him later today when I was home and when he got home I would visit him. During the course of the day, I had reached a decision. Allowing a man into my life was a scary proposition, but I knew I had to either do that or tell Vince it was never going to happen. When I looked at it from that angle, my choice was clear.

The thought of not seeing Vince again was worse than the concept of opening my heart to let him in. To be honest, the loveable rogue had already found a way past my defences, so it was more a case of accepting that my heart was where it belonged.

Needing Mindy to drive Vince's car – my right arm was in a sling – I turned around to find her saying goodbye to Lord Chamberlain

Not that they were exchanging words. Mindy's hands were locked around the back of his head and ... well, they were kissing. Let's leave it at that.

I sank into the passenger seat of the car, checked Amber and Buster were secure in the back, and when Mindy failed to appear more than a minute later, leaned across to toot the horn.

Mindy was blushing when she clambered behind the wheel. With an embarrassed grin on her face, she said, "Auntie, I think I'm in love."

THE FUTURE KING OF ENGLAND

"You know, Henkel, I think that went about as well as it could have."

Lord Chamberlain's little dachshund watched his human wander around the room.

"She's a feisty little thing. She'll certainly keep me entertained for a while. Not exactly the right class to marry the future king of England, obviously, but a worthwhile distraction since she is necessary."

Sitting on the edge of the bed to pet his dog, Lord Chamberlain chose to explain his thinking.

"You see, Henkel, I need Mindy to get me close to Mrs Philips and thus the royal wedding. A few of my family are going to meet with unfortunate accidents over the next few months but the wedding is the best opportunity to whittle them down."

"All those royals gathered in one place. It's just too good of an opportunity to miss. I need to decide how best to kill them all. I could go with a bomb, but the security people will be looking for that. Poison gas might be a fun option."

"I guess we shall see. Whatever I choose, Mindy is the key to get me inside and now all I have to do is play the part of the perfect boyfriend. Such a shame she'll have to die at the event too. That way I get to grieve and pull on the public heartstrings to gather support and recognition. I should be second in line to the throne by then if all goes to plan."

"Hmm, what was that Henkel?" Lord Chamberlain pretended to hear his dog speak. "What does that make you? Well, if I'm king, I think you'll probably be at least a duke, don't you?"

Henkel had no idea what his human was saying but wagged his tail obediently, nevertheless.

EPILOGUE

M any miles from the palace, amidst the chaotic destruction of a living room recently subject to an explosion of fury, a woman with murder in her eyes glared at her reflection in the mirror.

"Felicity Philips!" she seethed. There were cuts on her arm where she'd chosen to self-harm rather than take her rage out on another person. Sticky plasma leaked from her cuts where they were already beginning to heal.

"Felicity Philips? It should have been me! First that dirty slapper, Primrose Green got the job, and when I made sure the world knows what kind of woman she is, they go and give it to Felicity Philips! Are they all idiots? I was always the best wedding planner for the job!"

"Well, don't you worry," she glared down at a glossy magazine with Prince Marcus and Miss Morley on the cover, "I'll be throwing a spanner in her works, you mark my word. If this wedding even takes place it will be a miracle."

The End

AUTHOR'S NOTE:

H ello,

Thank you for reading this book. It is the sixth in this series and the eightieth overall. Shortly I will start on the next one and have the next ten or so lined up in my head.

Eighty books sounds like a silly number, an unachievable number until one realises that you just keep writing one chapter at a time, one book at a time, they add up whether you want them to or not.

Soon it will be one hundred stories crafted by my fair hand and that's just ridiculous.

This series of books will end at number ten. I have no plan to continue it after that, but there might be appearances in other stories for Felicity and her pets and a spin-off series with just the pets is entirely possible. I guess we shall see.

SOMETHING STOLEN, SOMETHING BLUE

In this book I employ the phrase 'at sixes and sevens' This is a common English idiom used to describe a condition of confusion or disarray.

I cannot say what happened to the Queen's corgis following her death, but feel certain they were taken care of in a manner befitting that which they were used to. I usually research such things, but decided I needed them to be at Buckingham Palace regardless. Two of the Queen's final corgis were called Sandy and Candy.

I have never taken afternoon tea at Claridge's and the closest I ever came to visiting the famous hotel was in 2022 when I almost had a meeting with an America TV executive looking to turn my Blue Moon series into a show. The meeting didn't happen and neither has the show, but who knows what the future could hold.

I have enjoyed afternoon tea at the Ritz though and the feast Mindy endures was precisely what I ate with my wife. It was at a time before children and we could get away with such things.

There are a few characters I used who you might not be familiar with if this is somehow your first book by me or you have ignored my Blue Moon and Patricia Fisher series.

Jane Butterworth is one of the detectives at the Blue Moon Investigation Agency which occupies a spot just along Rochester High Street from Felicity's boutique. Jane meets DI Cassie Munroe in a story called Sparks in the Darkness. It covers an escapade at the palace in which Eddie kills his brother, Nugent and looks to have gotten away with it.

Patricia Fisher also gets a mention. She is my most important character to date and the one who ties all the others together. A middle-aged English sleuth of Miss Marple calibre, she hired Felicity to plan her wedding and they have been friends ever since.

Jane and Patricia will pop up again in this series as we come to the grand finale. The royal wedding, as you have probably gathered, is going to be messed with by more than one party. To overcome this, in the final book a whole raft of my characters from different series will find themselves drawn into a single storyline.

I cannot express sufficiently how excited I am to write it.

One penalty of intertwining multiple series is that I managed to create two characters with the same first name. Lord Edward Chamberlain and Edward Smallbridge created an opportunity to really confuse readers. Hopefully, because they are never together and I employ Eddie for one character, I was able to minimise any head scratching.

I think that about covers it.

Take care.

Steve Higgs

WHAT'S NEXT FOR FELICITY AND FRIENDS?

Marriage? It can be absolute murder.

The royal wedding looms and Felicity can think of little else ... until a member of her dream team is arrested for attempted murder.

Veronica, a long-time friend and superstar florist, stands accused of attempting to kill half a dozen brides, their bouquets poisoned with an unknown toxin.

Ordered not to interfere by the hateful Chief Inspector Quinn, Felicity is determined to find the real person behind the bizarre crimes and clear her friend's name – Veronica must be innocent, right?

But Felicity is not exactly known for her sleuthing skills. If anything, she is known for the opposite. Accompanied by a P.I. with a shark-infested smile, a niece who likes to kick first and ask later, deluded dog, Buster, and sassy cat, Amber, it will be a miracle if she even finds a clue.

Time is running out for the brides – they need an antidote and fast.

However, in a race to save the day, Felicity will glimpse the truth and be faced with a choice that might change her life or end it.

What does a wedding planner know about solving a mystery?

Nothing.

Absolutely nothing.

Free Books and More

W ant to see what else I have written?

Go to my website -

Or sign up to my newsletter where you will get sneak peaks, exclusive giveaways, behind the scenes content, and more. Plus, you'll be notified of Fan Pricing events when they occur and get exclusive offers from other authors because all UF writers are automatically friends.

Click the link or copy it carefully into your web browser.

https://stevehiggsbooks.com/newsletter/

Prefer social media? Join my thriving Facebook community.

Want to join the inner circle where you can keep up to date with everything? This is a free group on Facebook where you can hang out with likeminded individuals and enjoy discussing my books. There is cake too (but only if you bring it).

https://www.facebook.com/groups/1151907108277718

ABOUT THE AUTHOR

At school, the author was mostly disinterested in every subject except creative writing, for which, at age ten, he won his first award. However, calling it his first award suggests that there have been more, which there have not. Accolades may come but, in the meantime, he is having a ball writing mystery stories and crime thrillers and claims to have more than a hundred books forming an unruly queue in his head as they clamour to get out. He lives in the south-east corner of England with a duo of lazy sausage dogs. Surrounded by rolling hills, brooding castles, and vineyards, he doubts he will ever leave, the beer is just too good.

Milton Keynes UK
Ingram Content Group UK Ltd.
UKHW021819280823
427632UK00010B/1097

9 781915 757708